She Holds Up the Stars

Sandra Laronde

annick
press

toronto · berkeley

We acknowledge the support of the Canada Council for the Arts and the
Ontario Arts Council, and the participation of the Government of Canada/
la participation du gouvernement du Canada for our publishing activities.

ONTARIO ARTS COUNCIL
CONSEIL DES ARTS DE L'ONTARIO
an Ontario government agency
un organisme du gouvernement de l'Ontario

Library and Archives Canada Cataloguing in Publication

Title: She holds up the stars / Sandra Laronde.
Names: Laronde, Sandra, author.
Identifiers: Canadiana (print) 20210335289 | Canadiana (ebook) 20210335335 |
ISBN 9781773210667 (hardcover) | ISBN 9781773210650 (softcover) |
ISBN 9781773210681 (HTML) | ISBN 9781773210674 (PDF)
Subjects: LCGFT: Novels.
Classification: LCC PS8623.A76347 S54 2022 | DDC jC813/.6—dc23

Published in the U.S.A. by Annick Press (U.S.) Ltd.
Distributed in Canada by University of Toronto Press.
Distributed in the U.S.A. by Publishers Group West.

Printed in Canada

annickpress.com
Also available as an e-book.
Please visit annickpress.com/ebooks for more details.

*To my mother Barbara
and my father Willis Laronde.
First and foremost.*

Chapter One

The last thing Misko wanted was to move away from the city. But her dreams, those strange visions, were rooted here and kept tugging at her to come home. Now that she was standing at Kokum's door, she wasn't sure she had made the right decision. But there was no turning back.

She remembered the door was never locked, so she gently pushed it open and pulled her bags inside. "Kokum?" she whispered. "Kokum?" she repeated a bit louder. An elderly woman shuffled toward her. "Kokum? It's me, Miskobimizh," she said, peering into her grandmother's face. Kokum hadn't looked this old six years ago. Her cheeks still pushed up against her eyes when she smiled. She did seem a bit shorter though, or maybe it was because

Misko was now 12 and had grown so much. The woman reached out her wrinkled hands, first placing them on Misko's shoulders and then gently touching her cheek.

It was the same cheek that still seemed to sting from the months-old slap. After it had happened, Misko was surprised there was no red hand imprinted on her face. Right now, in front of her grandmother, she instinctively sucked in the air between her teeth. She had developed this strange habit since the slap, her breath getting caught in her throat whenever she thought of that troubling time—or anything stressful for that matter.

"Here you are. Little Chickadee, you're such a big girl now," her grandmother murmured. And Misko relaxed a little, recognizing her childhood nickname and Kokum's soft voice. A pot was on the stove with a stew waiting to be heated. She saw two bowls and a loaf of bread on the counter. "Thank you, Kokum. I didn't feel like eating on the bus."

Misko liked that she was now old enough to take this trip alone—but the night of the slap was still very much in her memory. She was feeling a little nervous but had said nothing to Auntie Madeleine.

Of course, I'm sure, Misko had said. *I'm not a baby.*

Definitely not a baby anymore. Auntie Madeleine had sighed.

Still, baby or not, Auntie Madeleine arranged for the bus driver to watch over Misko and to make sure that she sat close to him, up front on the bus. He was the same bus driver who used to drive a young Madeleine between Winnipeg and Caribou Lake for holidays for many years.

Starting to feel hungry now, Misko turned on the burner and stirred. Every time she turned around, her grandmother was watching her. "We usually make this stew with moose meat, but we got none right now," said Kokum. Misko filled the bowls and carried them to the table.

"Maddy still like to cook?" asked Kokum as they sat down at the table.

"Yes, but she doesn't let me help." Misko sighed. "She said she can do it faster if she does it herself."

Kokum huffed. "Always bossy, that one."

Auntie Madeleine had said nothing to Kokum about starting a new job with longer hours. The kitchen looked like something staged for a catalog, not a place where you prepared food. Likewise, Misko said nothing about how Auntie had cut her own long hair short, gotten a whole new wardrobe of silk blouses and stylish pantsuits, or started coming home long past suppertime. They began ordering a lot of takeout back in Winnipeg, which was exciting at first, but Misko missed homemade meals. On the weekends, when her aunt would sometimes use the kitchen, she would shoo Misko away whenever she asked to help.

Kokum looked directly into her eyes. "And how about you, dear? Are you still a fast runner?"

"Pretty fast," replied Misko with a shrug.

Kokum nodded, motioning to a wall unit in the corner. Misko went to look and there she was: young Maddy, her hair long and loose. Her self-assured smile was familiar but her face was softer somehow, more open. There were many other framed photos—in sepia, black and white, and color—but most were frameless snapshots. There were pictures of great grandparents, grandparents, aunts, uncles, sisters, brothers, siblings, children, babies, and pets.

"Wow, you have . . . I mean, *we* have such a big family, Kokum." Misko could see a familiar glint in her relatives' dark brown eyes. It was like looking at many versions of her own face, staring back at her across generations of time.

Then she came across a photo of two people who did not fit in at all. They were a fancy couple tossing a striped beach ball on a white sandy beach.

"Kokum, who's this?"

Kokum looked at the photo blankly for a moment, blinking as she tried to remember. "Oh, those white people, they came *with* the frame."

"You have a picture of people you don't even know?" asked Misko.

Kokum chuckled. "Not sure who goes in that frame yet," she replied.

Misko moved to the next photo. "Is this one here a picture of you, Kokum?"

"How do I look?"

"It's hard to tell because you look blurry."

"Must've been when I was young," Kokum said with a grin.

There was another photo that stood out to Misko. She picked it up. It was a picture of a young girl.

"That's your mom," said Kokum.

The girl was holding the reins of a brown and beige pony. A quiver ran up Misko's spine, but she didn't know why. "She . . . my mother had a horse?"

"Ah-hey."

The girl in the picture seemed about her age, but her hair was cut short and tucked behind her ears. Her eyes were bright and stared at whoever held the camera, and they seemed to look directly into Misko's at that exact moment. She felt a strange collapsing of time as if she and Mother were here together now, in this same room. Two 12-year-old girls, looking at each other across time.

"You remind me of her," said Kokum.

"I do?"

"Ah-hey."

"She looks happy. I didn't know she had a pony!"

Misko stared at the photo a little longer, then put it down and picked up another that had fallen sideways. Her mother was holding a baby and squinting into the sun. The shadow of whoever took the picture lay across the foreground, hovering over their bodies. "Is the baby me?"

Her grandmother contemplated the photograph.

Misko stood still, waiting impatiently for her to respond.

"Too small. So cute," Kokum finally said softly. Misko held her breath to hear. "A baby bird. Bineshiiwens. Nothing but a little chickadee. I love their song," she cooed.

So that's where my nickname comes from.

"I wonder how they fly south for the winter with such little wings?" Misko wondered aloud.

"Kawin, those birds don't fly south, m'girl. Them people build birdhouses in their backyards." Kokum drew the outline of a tiny box with her hands. "Them birds go right inside and what do they do? They build a nest. They build *round* inside. I don't know why the white man wants to put everything in a box. Even cut up our land into boxes. No, those birds don't leave. Not like people."

When her grandmother spoke again, the words seemed to float on the air as she exhaled. "Anna. Gone eight years."

"What's that, Kokum?"

But Kokum didn't answer, and Misko could feel the energy shift in the room. Kokum stood up slowly, turned, and wiped an invisible tear from her cheek. "Well, dear, I have to get some rest now." Misko's throat tightened as she watched Kokum amble down the hallway and into her room. She didn't remember her grandmother being sad like this the last time she was here.

It had been eight years since Misko's mom disappeared. Eight years of longing for her mother. Eight years of

Kokum waiting for good news of her daughter Anna. Eight years of people saying to let it go, to forget about it, and to move on. "But it's our loss, and it's still unsolved," said Auntie Madeleine.

Chapter Two

———✳———

Misko sat up in bed. She wondered why so much light was streaming into her room before she remembered where she was. She *never* got this kind of sunlight in her room back in Winnipeg. Tiny specks of dust danced in a shaft of sunlight, and she could hear birds chirping and singing outside.

She went into the kitchen and let the water run from the faucet for a minute. Once it was warm, she splashed a bit on her face to wake up more. She sipped some water and wondered whether the boil water alert was a thing here. Just in case, she boiled the water longer than usual before making tea for Kokum.

She moved into the living room and ran a wide-toothed comb through her hair; dividing it into three sections, she whispered the prayer she learned from Auntie Madeleine, who had learned it from Kokum. One section of the braid was Spirit, the second was Mind, and the third was Body—"Manitou, nendamowin, wiiyiw." She repeated the words over and over until her braid was done.

She pulled the braid over her left shoulder so it lay on her heart and she could fiddle with its end. Auntie Madeleine wasn't here after all to get cross at her for chewing on the end of it.

When the tea was brewed, Misko knocked on her grandmother's door, pushed the door open a smidge, and peered inside. "Kokum, I've made tea," she said. She paused for a moment and asked, "Whatcha listening to?" Kokum was sitting on the side of the bed listening to the lyrics of a familiar song. It was something about walking the line for someone you love.

The song was recognizable yet Misko couldn't place it. Something from her childhood that her mother had listened to? As the song ended, Kokum tapped twice on the edge of the ceramic mug with her spoon. *Clink, clink.* "Did Shoshana come home last night?"

"Shoshana?"

Kokum stood up and walked to the window. "The rain came down hard last night. Big wind, too. Everything got so charged up. The thunder beings rolled in and lit up the sky. Flash! Flash! Flash! 'Animikii,' that's what we call that happening. Did I ever tell you when your mom was little she used to go outside and laugh while the sky was lighting up—hee hee, that girl! Well, better get to my garden now and see how the wee ones are doing after the big storm."

Misko stood there blinking at her grandmother's story. She could almost see her mother's fresh young face and rosy cheeks and hear her laughing as each flash lit up the sky, rocks, and trees. Her breath caught a little and she remembered to exhale deeply.

She looked at the CD cover on the bedside table. Johnny Cash. Auntie Madeleine used to listen to him, too, and she knew her mother did as well—that was one of the few precious shards of knowledge she had of her mother from the small stories shared so hesitantly. *Why does everyone only tell me bits and pieces of the puzzle about my mom?*

She trailed behind her grandmother as she hobbled outside and wondered yet again if she'd made a mistake coming here. Before going outside, she grabbed the photo of her mom and herself as a baby. *Why did you leave me? Why haven't you come back?* No answer, of course. "We simply don't know," Auntie Madeleine had told her. "If she's one of the missing . . ." Her eyes fixed, unblinking, on some faraway point.

Misko had heard a bit about the Indigenous women and girls who had gone missing. Auntie Madeleine said that thousands of women and girls "never returned home," and that when Misko got older she should "never go on *that* highway out west in British Columbia." Misko's throat tightened. She remembered the stranger who tried to abduct her, coaxing her to come see the cute kittens in his car. The man had slapped her cheek hard to stop her from screaming for help. Now rubbing her cheek, Misko remembered her auntie forbidding her to walk around by herself after dark, stating that she didn't want Misko "to become *another statistic* like Anna." It was the main reason why Auntie sent her here for the summer.

Coming back to the reserve brought up a lot of memories of her missing mother. It felt so remote here—so isolated, and what could she possibly do on this rez? *Why do I even have to be here in the first place? I don't want to be here.*

Chapter Three

———❊———

While Kokum was outside digging in the garden, Misko explored the house. She found an unopened tin of Walker's Shortbread in a kitchen cupboard and decided cookies were as good a breakfast as anything else. She explored the house, cookies in hand, and discovered two more bedrooms. The house was square, but this patchwork place felt cozy and somehow round inside. *Probably because it feels loved.*

She opened the closet door of the first bedroom. A few clothes hung on wire hangers and an old, weathered shoebox lay on the floor. When she picked it up, it had weight. She sat on the mattress and lifted the lid as carefully as if she had unearthed a treasure chest.

On top were newspaper clippings showing photos taken in schools, with little kids sitting row upon row, all wearing uniforms. Ojibway and Cree children. Nuns stood at the back, their faces stern. Someone had written names in red ink across the bottom of several photos— Laura, Chun, Noodin, Flora. One photo was part of a full-length article. "Survivors Speak to Indian and Northern Affairs," read the headline. And with a sick feeling, Misko knew. They were official photos taken in residential schools. Auntie Madeleine had mentioned these terrible stories—stories about more than 150,000 children taken from their homes and families, forced to go to schools far away, and punished for being "Indian." Misko scanned the little kids' faces in the photos. Her eyes welled up as she pictured their little hearts aching to go home.

She remembered her auntie's words: "It happened to your mom, too, your grandfather, uncle Ziibi, and some of our other relatives. But, after . . . your mother disappeared, it all caught up with Kokum."

"So Kokum never went to residential school?" asked Misko.

"That's right. Luckily, she wasn't home on that fateful day when they came to scoop up the children. They probably never came back for her because she was the eldest child in her family. Younger children were preferred as they were much easier to break."

Misko was happy that her grandmother had been spared. *But my mother wasn't so lucky. It must have broken Kokum's heart to have her first-born daughter sent off to that awful school.*

"Auntie, how come you didn't have to go to residential school?"

"I'm seven years younger than Anna, your mom. Kokum hatched a plan and didn't register my birth to protect me from being scooped up. I was then sent to live with relatives in Winnipeg for a few years. One child taken away was already way too much for Kokum to bear."

Underneath the newspaper clippings were a pair of baby booties, a heart-shaped rock, and a silver ring with a turquoise stone. Misko put the lid back on the box and returned it to the closet, feeling like a trespasser, as if she had read someone else's diary. She tiptoed out and went to the other room. This room had a futon on a low frame and a dresser with drawers that squawked when she tugged them open. The drawers were invitingly empty and so was the closet. Misko made up her mind this would be her room for the summer.

She tugged on the window blind and when it didn't roll up, she yanked harder. It landed in a clump at her feet with a loud clatter. She pushed on the window frame until it opened and leaned out, looking across the yard, past the fence, and into the distance. Time looped backward and it was that otherworldly feeling again where her body tingled and time expanded. She was now looking into the biggest and most beautiful pair of eyes she had ever seen. The animal was both real and like something from a dream. And he was magnificent.

Then she listened intently. It sounded like a whinny at first and then a low-pitched voice followed by a nickering sound. It was a bit garbled and hard to make out at first, but then a soft "mish-ta" sound floated up into her awareness.

I wonder what "mish-ta" means.

Chapter Four

———◦✳◦———

A loud shout jolted Misko back to the here and now. A man on a large chestnut-colored horse charged over the hill, his arm raised, a whip in his hand, and a smaller, unsaddled horse ran ahead of him, barely escaping the abuse. *Whoosh!* The sound of air splitting apart. *Thwack!* The sound of the whip hitting the horse's flank. *Whoosh! Thwack!* Misko flinched, feeling the sting across her own shoulders.

The horse reared, let loose an ear-piercing scream, and galloped up the hill. With a gasp of relief, Misko saw the man veer in another direction. She scrambled over the windowsill and ran across the scrub to the wooden fence. A boy stood some ways off, holding another whip, staring at the treeline, his eyes narrowed and searching.

"Hey!" Her shout pierced the air as she clambered over the fence rails. "Hey you!"

He swung around to face her, an annoyed look on his face. "Who are you?"

"I live here," Misko answered, jumping down and then walking toward him.

"No you don't. You're on my property. So, you *don't* live *here.*"

He had blond hair and blue eyes with lots of lashes and stood half a head taller than Misko. And the scowl on his face dared her to insult him.

"Not *here* here, stupid," she said. "There." She flung out her arm, pointing. "Over there."

"The reserve? Well then, go back there-over-there. I'm busy."

"Doing what?"

"Did you see that horse? You must've seen it. I'm busy with the horse."

"Oh, you're busy all right, busy hurting a horse," she snapped, putting her hand on her hip. "You and that man."

"It's *our* horse and it's none of your beeswax."

"Why? Why do you have to hurt a horse? It's stupid."

"You're the stupid one," he answered. "We're breaking him. Me and my dad. That's why."

"So, you admit it!" Misko said. "You *are* hurting him. *Breaking* him!"

"I have to break him!" he shouted, flinging his arms up in anger. "It's my job to train him, and I can't do that if he isn't scared of me. Okay?"

"No! It's not okay. Maybe you could *train* him if he *wasn't* afraid of you." She was so tight with anger she trembled. Her breath became shallow and quick. There was no way hitting a horse was the right way to get him to obey.

The boy's face flushed. "I can't train him until I break him. What don't you get?"

"You. I don't get *you*!" Misko glared at the boy. "Why do you have to *break* everything anyway?" she shouted. She thought of the man who slapped her and how he had tried to break her, too.

"What do you mean?"

"My aunt says people break things. They break everything. They break up, break down, and they break promises. And now I see you breaking horses, too. Why do you have to break everything? Why can't you leave things alone?" She turned her back and walked toward the fence. *Breaking promises?* Why was she taking all of this out on that stupid boy? He didn't get it anyway!

"Whatcha talking about?" the boy shouted back, and she turned around. "You live over there with that old woman, don't you? My dad says she's crazy!" He put his finger to his head and twirled it. *"Cray-cray."*

Misko climbed over the fence and faced him from the other side. "My grandmother is *not* crazy! Probably one of the smartest people you'll *never* know. What's wrong with *you*?"

She didn't wait for him to answer. She took off running. Back home in Winnipeg, she was the fastest on her track team and could outrun any boy her age. She loved to run. It was the one place where she could shine. If it weren't for her natural athleticism, she'd feel mostly invisible as an Indigenous kid—not seen, not heard, and definitely not remembered. She'd put up her hand in class surrounded by white classmates and teachers, only to be ignored, even though she was flesh and bone. The kids taunted her at school because of her skin color and for being Indigenous. They would pretend to shoot her with a bow and arrow, run away from her and call her "stink-bomb," accuse her if anything was stolen, or say she cheated if she got an A on a test. Like death by a thousand cuts, it had all started to wear her down even though she was just 12 years old. She sensed that people didn't expect much from her and this made her feel sad. But she did have something that she loved back in Winnipeg. She had the track team and running made her feel powerful. Running made her feel visible. Running made her feel like a star. So, right now, she ran as fast as she could. Up the hill, away from the boy, away from Kokum's house. Running. Like the horse.

Like my mother.

Chapter Five

———◆✳◆———

Misko collapsed somewhere along the fence. The same fence that kept that boy on his side, on *his* property. She dropped to her knees, her lungs burning and thrusting fire into her throat. When her breathing slowed, she lay on her back and closed her eyes, stretching out her arms, hands, and fingers at her sides. Underneath her, she felt the furry fuzz of moss growing in patches here and there, thrusting up out of rock—granite—the oldest rock in the world. She had learned about the Canadian Shield from one of those books her auntie used to read to her when she was a little girl, when there were no stylish pantsuits, when there was more time, and when they spent Sundays at the library.

She still went to the library on Sunday afternoons by herself, reading all she could on nature but mostly leafing through big coffee table books full of pictures of art. There was one teacher, Mrs. Reed, who had said that Misko was "very perceptive" and could often make observations that other kids her age could not see or understand. Misko clung to those few kind words because Mrs. Reed was the first teacher who showed any real interest in her. That same favorite teacher said she had an ability to "connect the dots"—whatever that meant. It was from the library books that she learned about her auntie's favorite painters. One of them, Benjamin Chee Chee from Bear Island on Lake Temagami, spent many years searching for his mother, too. And Norval Morrisseau from the Indian Group of Seven, who painted lines not seen by the human eye, lines that connected everything. *It was like he had X-ray vision*, Misko had thought. She loved the gorgeous colors of those paintings—and some of the colors she could only ever see in her dreams—from the sun-burning yellows to piercing turquoise blues to sharp burnt oranges and reds. She liked the boldly colorful abstract work of Daphne Odjig, too, and how she showed the guts and grace of Anishinaabe people and their land.

Remembering all of those brushstrokes of color made Misko feel at home in these woodlands. She relaxed her body as she felt the grooves and ridges of the earth beneath her. And, for the first time in her life, she felt the land embrace and cradle her.

Home. The word seeped in and flooded her thoughts— *home, home, home.* The sounds, the light, the smell, all felt like *home.*

We're swirling through the air, brown hands gripping my small wrists so tight, swinging me in a wide circle, light as a feather. "Ninga, Mama!" 'Round and 'round we go. I look up and see the treetops, the sky, and my mother's long dark hair swirling above me. We twirl until we get dizzy and collapse on the ground—on this land—and my mother, Anna, hugs me into her body, her head on mine, and the two of us gasping, laughing.

Misko opened her eyes, and the memory slipped away. She sat up and breathed in the warmth and freshness of the morning light until she didn't know where she ended and the beauty began—the robin's egg sky, black tadpoles transforming into a frog's moss green, the sparse lime-emerald grass not yet burned brown by the summer sun. The blackflies were over, and the mosquitoes were napping, but still there was a humming all about her as if the air crackled with life.

And when she turned her head, she saw *him.*

He was grazing on the other side of the fence, relaxed, without a drop of fear. His black tail swished.

She moved slowly to stand and leaned on the fence. She hadn't been up close to a horse like this in years—

unsaddled, unharnessed. *Unhumaned.* The horses she saw in Winnipeg were scary RCMP horses that towered over her with cold-faced police officers in the saddle. The horses' tails did not swing freely but were braided with ribbons, decorated for a fair, like little girls going to a party.

Now that she could get a better look, she gazed at the long lean legs, the powerful brown body, the black mane and matching tail. She observed the graceful curve of his neck, and when he lifted his magnificent head, his nostrils widened, inhaling her scent. He tossed his head, swished his tail, and for a few moments, they stood quietly together, girl and horse. She sensed a shiver in him—not the kind that she could see but something pulsating and so alive inside the horse that it reverberated in her, too. He had so much light in his big beautiful brown eyes. It looked like he swallowed the moon whole. *I could swim in those eyes,* she thought. *Get washed away.* The horse lowered his head in search of a clump of anything green, stopped mid-chew for a moment, and then went back to munching on whatever he found tasty.

She stood a few meters away, patiently waiting for him to make the first move. Then, without lifting his head, he sidled closer and closer. With his every step, he became more curious about her. Then Misko watched her arm rise up, without her mind telling it to, as if there was no gravity, weightless and effortless. She held her hand below the horse's nose. "Hi," she whispered. "Nice to meet you." The horse's ears twitched ever so slightly. He nickered and blew a puff of warm air on the back of her hand. The breath from his big nostrils tickled as he stepped in closer and brushed his nose against her hand. "Good boy," she said softly, and her heart leapt in excitement. She rubbed him again. "Good horse," she said, pouring as much love into her touch as she could muster. Then his name rose up in her thoughts—"Mishta . . . Mishta . . . shta . . . shta . . . Mishtadim," she whispered aloud.

The horse lowered his head to her chest. "Mish-ta-dim," she said again, this time pronouncing the syllables as if teaching him Anishinaabemowin. "That's your name, Mish-ta-dim. That's what I'll call you." She stroked him, running the flat of her palm down his neck and shoulder, caressing the cascade of his black mane. "You're a real beauty, Mishtadim." His ears twitched forward as if saying *I like, I like*, and his tail swooshed behind him as an echo. *Me too, me too.*

She whispered his name again: "Mishtadim." She touched her own ponytail. "I have a mane, too, just like you. Look, we have matching hairstyles." It was silly talk, but Mishtadim didn't seem to mind. "You like me talking to you, don't you, Mishtadim?" For an answer, he pushed his nostrils into her shoulder, inhaling her scent.

She heard the sudden flapping of wings and to her right three grouse stumbled from the brush and hop-skipped into clumsy low flight. Mishtadim's head shot up, jerking to one side, and he pulled back, his eyes wild.

"It's okay, Mishtadim! They're birds. Only birds."

But he was gone. Running uphill, bucking the fear off his body.

Misko looked at her hand, marveling that she had touched this creature. No. That wasn't quite right. He had *accepted* her touch.

Chapter Six

———————✳———————

The next day, Misko went to the same spot at the fence where she'd encountered Mishtadim, hoping to see him again. Or even the boy. If the boy was around, maybe Mishtadim would be, too. She'd tell him about how she talked to Mishtadim and that she could do a better job of training him, no problem.

She followed the fence up the hill, past where she'd seen Mishtadim, and down to a small lake—Cross Lake, she remembered the name as she approached it—where the fence disappeared.

Along the shore were docks with boats tied to posts, canoes pulled up onshore, and leading away from the boats were paths to homes. Where she stood, low blueberry bushes heavy with unripe berries grew out of gray rock. And next to them were thickets of blackberry canes, their berries still small, red, and sour.

She heard a shout and looked to see someone waving from a group of kids by the lake. "Hey, you're Misko, aren't you?" a boy's voice called out.

She chewed nervously on her bottom lip while scanning the kids' faces; they were mostly her age. "Yes, I am," she shouted, waving back. She remembered playing with these kids six years ago, but what would they be like now?

"Misko! Ambe omaa, come join us!"

She waited a moment longer and then jumped down the rocks and saw that they were sitting in a circle of folding lawn chairs with an upside-down galvanized tub in the middle. They were pretending to play the big drum like adult men in the arbor at the powwow, where women would gather 'round to sing.

"How's it going?" He was a tall and heavy boy, with a smidge of a mustache, and he wore a faded navy-blue T-shirt. He looked nothing like the little boy she had played with as a child, but she recognized him instantly.

"Nelson?"

A blazing white smile lit his face. "Geez, you remembered!"

"'Course she remembers, doofus. She's probably been dreaming about you all these years." The other boy winked at her and Nelson punched him in the arm. "Nimkii's the name," he added, rubbing the spot where he'd been punched. "I came home a year ago. Best thing ever."

Misko smiled apprehensively and looked around the circle. "Uh . . . hi, Sage. Autumn, hi. Kiiwedin, hi. Sadie, hi. Geez, everyone's so grown-up." Last time she spent time with these kids they had played hide-and-seek and argued over who'd get to be captain of the spaceship or leader of the wolf pack. None of the kids back then knew that the land next to the rez was occupied by an angry white man who broke horses.

Kokum had still waited in her comfy old chair with the TV on every night, still hoping her daughter would come back. Mr. Turner's one-stop grocery store had just reopened after renovations, serving both rez and ranch residents. She remembered he'd kept four old ponies grazing peacefully out back. She recalled Nelson's chubby legs barely gripping the horse's wide back as he was only four years old at the time.

"Sit here," a tiny young girl said as she squished to the side of her lawn chair. "I'm Kiera."

"Have you done any singing before?" Nimkii asked.

"Not really," Misko said, shrugging.

"Someday I want to be a lead singer of the big drum and do the powwow circuit all over Turtle Island," Nimkii said eagerly.

"We're creating round dance songs and trying to

remember some of the old songs, too," Sage chimed in. Misko noticed how pretty she was, as pretty as her cousins Haley and Katie, and her older cousin Autumn seemed so tall now.

Nimkii started a drumbeat in the *thump, thump. . . thump, thump* heartbeat rhythm, singing underneath his breath to remind everyone what song they were about to sing. Without missing a beat, he assumed the demeanor of his uncles, speaking sombrely: "The drum is very powerful. It's the heartbeat of our nation and the heartbeat of our Mother the Earth." He beamed. "We try to match our heartbeat to Hers and the drum helps us to do that."

"Ah, she doesn't need a big speech, just sing the song, will ya!" Nelson teased.

"Don't worry about him," Nimkii said with a wink. "One day, he'll be able to sing *almost* as good as me. He just can't quite hit those high notes yet, ayeee!"

Nelson countered in friendly competition and sang the highest note that he could, "Yaaaa," and when his voice cracked, he erupted in a fit of coughing and everyone laughed.

"Ahem," Nimkii said as he cleared his throat. "This song that I'm about to sing is special. Like my buddy Nelson over there." He gave a nod to the smiling boy. "This song came to my grandfather in a dream, so here goes." Nimkii started to wail the old song, and the drumming rose up and grabbed hold of Misko's heart and wouldn't let go. It held her in its firm grip. She tried to escape the sound by adjusting herself, moving her body, but it just wouldn't shake loose. It rattled around and then broke up something inside, and surprisingly, tears streamed down her cheeks. She just couldn't stop crying. She closed her eyes so that the others wouldn't notice her tears. She could hear Nimkii's voice and drumbeats thumping inside of her chest, and everything around her became one snapshot in time where the past, present, and future met as one. She could see energy patterns in constant motion like a kaleidoscope where invisible lines made of love connected everything. She felt it all—the streams that washed against rocks, the loons that called, the fish that splashed, and a red squirrel scolded her kits in the drey. She felt the joy and freedom in that connection. She didn't have the words to describe this moment, but she had a deeply felt sense that all things were perpetually unfolding, whether human or nonhuman, animate or inanimate, the here and now or forever.

Suddenly, Misko thought of her auntie's favorite painting back home. She remembered its vibrant colors and how she loved to trace the dark contours and lines with her forefinger as a child. She traced fish underwater to people in a canoe to geese flying overhead and all the way up to the bright sun. These dark lines connected everything, and she could circle back and trace them all over again and again. She thought that she was just tracing lines back then, but in this moment, it felt as though she had climbed inside of that painting and traced everything again. But this time, it was with a knowingness of where everything belonged. No, where *everyone* belonged—whether it be tree, rock, sun, human, or insect— all interconnected by a web of invisible lines.

Now, looking up from her seated position, she saw the kids' faces hovering over her.

"Misko?" whispered Kiera. "Misko, are you okay?" She gripped her hand tightly. Misko wiped her eyes with her sleeve. "Sorry. I . . . I get like this sometimes."

"I get it. Ever awful us; we made a girl cry," Nelson teased.

Misko smiled. "Naw, it's just the drum made me feel . . ."

"It's okay. The drum does that to people. It wakes up something inside," Nimkii said.

"It's your ancestors that you feel," Sage added. "You realize that they were always there."

"Can I get you a drink of water?" Kiera asked.

Misko shook her head. "I'm sorry if I ruined everything."

"You're crazy," Nimkii joked gently. "We know you cried at my brilliance." He put up his hand to high-five Nelson but then quickly took his hand away just when Nelson was about to slap his palm.

"Psych," Nimkii taunted him.

"You owe me a high-five," Nelson jibed back, and everyone laughed, including Misko.

They ate chips and everyone asked Misko about living in Winnipeg, and then Nelson said he could drive her back to Kokum's. "That's my ATV over there. Want a lift?"

"Ever big show-off, you." Nimkii swatted him playfully.

When Nelson punched him again, Nimikii pretended to fall off his lawn chair, and Misko giggled. After saying goodbye to the others, she hopped on the ATV. "I can drive you straight home or we can go by the store," said Nelson. "Mr. Turner hates us kids making so much noise. Sometimes we buzz him on purpose."

"Just home would be great. Thank you, I mean . . . miigwetch."

She wondered why they tried to upset Mr. Turner and if he still let kids ride his ponies. When she was little, kids paid 50 cents for a pony ride on the frozen lake at the winter carnival. Mr. Turner might remember her because she once went on five rides in a row and even remarked on how much she loved horses. He even gave her one free ride. The memory sparkled brightly, as if it was just the other day. She recalled how kind he had been, towering over her as he gave her a leg up on the pony. He had helped her—but would he even recognize her now? How she had loved those winter carnivals back then—dogsled races, log-sawing contests, the best ice sculptures, weight-pulling contests for dogs, snowshoe and snowmobile races, and even a Snow Queen beauty pageant. Misko remembered when she was five that Auntie Madeleine had won the beauty contest. But, then again, she was the *only* one who'd entered. Everyone else was too shy. Nonetheless, Auntie Madeleine had moxie and brought home a big, shiny trophy, purple and gold with a regal woman on top holding a scepter. How she loved to brag about winning the trophy, but she always left out the part about being the only contestant. This fond memory made Misko smile, but then she frowned; she really did miss her confident auntie back in Winnipeg.

Misko clambered off the ATV at the trail to Kokum's.

"How long you staying for?" Nelson asked. "The summer? Forever and ever?"

"Just for . . ."

His eyes crinkled into a big smile.

"I'm staying just for the summer and then I'll be back in Winnipeg to start school in the fall."

Chapter Seven

———•❊•———

Misko turned off the light and looked out the window. It wasn't very dark. She opened the door and stepped outside and looked up.

Stars!

The light was from the stars and the moon, millions of stars pulsing in the sky, some as tiny as pinpricks in what looked like a trail of spilled milk in the sky. She never looked up at the night sky in Winnipeg. There wasn't much to see—just a whole lot of fuzziness from too much light pollution. Why would you even bother looking up? But here you couldn't help but *look up*.

She remembered Kokum telling her about the Milky Way, which was a pathway—a river of souls—making their journey home.

"We call it Jibaykana, my dear. We don't say Milky Way in our language; that's what the white man calls it. We would never call it the *Milky* Way because, well, most of us are—what's that fancy word in English?—lack . . . toss?"

"Lactose intolerant?"

"Ah-hey," Kokum nodded.

Misko leaned against the railing and tilted her head back and stared until her eyes watered and the stars swam closer together. She thought about how stars have a life. They are born, they get older, and they disappear. *Just like her mother.*

A big bat flew across her vision, and a small animal cried out, startled, and was cut off so quickly that Misko was frightened. She went back inside, brushed her teeth, and changed for bed. She lay down and closed her eyes and within minutes was asleep.

In a dream, I walk along the shoreline of a big body of water. I don't just hear the waves, I let the sound splash inside my chest. With each wave lapping at my feet, it fills my spirit and straightens my spine. I know that I have to get to the other side somehow. I spot a large birchbark canoe by the shore and get in. The man in the stern of the canoe is someone I am related to, but I'm not sure how. The entire dream is in Anishinaabemowin, the Ojibway language, and all my thoughts are in Anishinaabemowin. I understand every single spoken word and every single thought. I discover that the man's name is Noodin.

I have traveled a great distance and I am thirsty and hungry. I take a sip of water and am overcome with a strong sense of familiarity of this place. Even the sweet taste of water is familiar. The shoreline, the trees and rock, are all recognizable. I know that I have somehow entered into "old time." Deep time. A different time. Not clock time.

When the canoe reaches its destination, the man smiles at me and wishes me well as I step out onto the shore. There is a person waiting in the shadow of a tree, someone who is expecting me. I can feel that this person loves me very much and sense that it's a woman who has waited a long time. On coming closer, I am greeted by a beautiful woman with flowing dark hair and brown eyes who wears wide bracelets on both wrists, made out of hefty silver, turquoise, and leather. When I look more closely at one of the bracelets, I notice that a little piece of gemstone is missing from the center of the bracelet and that the bracelet covers the raised line of a scar.

Chapter Eight

The next morning, Misko helped Kokum in the garden. Since there was so little soil on top of all the granite, Kokum used large round clay pots filled with earth, and chicken wire kept out rabbits, squirrels, and chipmunks. She picked little bugs off the cucumbers and pinched off side shoots on the tomato plants. Green beans grew inches overnight and had to be retied to sticks daily.

"What's that?" Misko asked, pointing to dark green leaves with a red spine down the middle.

"Rhubarb."

"Ick. I hate rhubarb." She made a face. "Rank."

"Rank?"

"Gross, Kokum. It means gross."

"Your mother liked it. Sometimes ate it raw with a bit of sugar, like this." Kokum motioned dipping a rhubarb stalk into a bowl of sugar and then biting off its end. Misko's expression soured as if she had actually tasted it, and Kokum laughed. She reached over, her nails caked with earth, and tweaked Misko's chin.

"Well, if my mom liked it, I guess I could give it a shot. I've never actually had it."

"Atta girl."

Misko looked around. "There sure are lots of weeds around here, Kokum. Do you want me to pull them out for you?"

"Those aren't weeds, my girl. That's mashkiki."

"Huh?"

"Medicine. Mashkiki. Every plant has a gift. You just have to know how to see its gift to release it. You see these yellow ones here? Shiiwaniibish, whatchamacallit in English . . . dan-de-lions. Mashkiki." Misko looked around and saw hundreds of dandelions nodding their yellow heads in agreement with Kokum. "So much medicine 'round here. Onizhiishin. It's good. You see here, you can eat these all the way down to their roots."

"Ick."

"See these dark green leaves?" Kokum's index finger outlined a deep-toothed one. "They're good for the kidneys. Odikosiw, that's our word for kidneys." She touched Misko's back in her upper abdominal area. "The flower part is good for the liver. Okonima," Kokum continued as she took Misko's hands and placed them on the upper right side of her own abdomen above her stomach. "This flower cleans your blood."

Misko never really thought about flowers cleaning anything, let alone eating them. *How does Kokum know all this anyway?* Back in school, she remembered coloring the different parts of human anatomy in biology class, but she never thought of these vital organs being inside of her body, beneath her own skin. They had seemed abstract, tucked in a book, and somehow on the outside of her, until now.

Kokum brought in two handfuls of dandelion flowers, stems, leaves, and roots inside the house for drying. "Tea time," she said, motioning Misko to come inside.

The girl hesitated, her attention on a big tree behind the house that had hundreds of pine cones weighing down its branches. "Kokum, what kind of tree is that over there?"

"M'girl, trees are not a *what;* they are a *who.* Mitig, that's how we say tree in our language. Mitig is alive like us. They talk to one another, and you can talk to them, too. You see how some of them are bent this way or that way or even look a bit odd? That's because they didn't get enough light. Mitig doesn't judge that they're too this or too that. They just turned out that way is all. Kind of like people. And you see that mitig over there?" she added, pointing with a quick pursing of her lips. "That tree is suckering, growing sideways and all over the place because it got too much light. It didn't know which way to grow. It didn't have bigger trees to make a path of light to help it grow straight up, in the right direction. Now, these trees here grow almost anywhere and everywhere, even on rock. They are zhingwaak. In English, they call them jack pine."

For the rest of the morning, Misko followed her grandmother around as she tended to the plants.

Later on, Misko helped tidy up around the house. She dusted the wall unit and went through all the photos again, determined to ask her grandmother about who everyone was—maybe put labels on the back of the photos—when she thought about the contents of the shoebox.

Before bed, Misko went outside to see if she could spot a shooting star. Sometimes she was able to pick out a constellation. The Big Dipper was super easy to spot, and she read once that there were more stars than grains of sand on earth. She really couldn't understand how anyone—like those ancient astronomers—could find patterns and make sense of them all. She had heard that you could navigate your way home by the North Star. She felt a kind of gravitational pull from the stars. The kind of pull that never gets talked about in school. An ancestral pull. And when she blinked, the stars seem to blink back.

She looked across the yard and into the distance, hoping that Mishtadim would appear. She missed him. When it got too chilly, she went back inside and marveled at the stars from the warmth of her bedroom window. *I wonder how my ancestors saw the stars when there weren't telescopes back then? How did they know so much about them?*

Misko drew the makeshift curtain. Outside, a shadow moved from the dark of the bushes along the path. Her heart pounded. She watched as someone climbed the front steps and put a hand on the doorknob.

The door wasn't locked. She bolted out of her room to meet the intruder, blood rushing to her head, her heart wild in her chest.

Chapter Nine

——❋——

A girl stepped inside, wiping her feet, shrugging off a denim jacket. She was pretty with short light brown hair tucked behind her ears and looked younger than Misko. She walked confidently with her shoulders pulled back and made herself at home on the sofa. She only looked out of place once she noticed Misko.

"Oh! You must be Misko!" she said. "I knew you were coming so I should've knocked first, but people don't knock on doors around here. I just got back from Bobbie's camp and was worried about Kokum—it's been a few nights since I've checked in," she added quickly. She spoke in a rush, each word tumbling over the next. "I guess if you don't need me here, I'll get going." Not waiting for an answer, the girl backed up until she was standing in the doorway.

"Stop! Who are you?" Misko turned on a light to get a better look at her.

"Oh! I'm Shoshana."

"Shoshana?" Misko remembered her grandmother asking about a Shoshana. "Are you another granddaughter?" Misko wondered if this girl with her round green eyes was a relative she didn't know about. "Are you here to visit?"

"My mother sends me here to sleep."

"To sleep? Why would you come here to sleep?"

"Oh! When my own grandmother died, it was just my mom, my dad, and me. Your Kokum took me in and adopted me so I could grow up with a grandmother. My dad is white and my mom is Native, so Mom thought that it would be good for me to learn some of the old ways."

"So, you're adopted in?"

"You bet. 'Indian-style' adopted in," she said, her fingers making air quotes. "That was, oh . . . three years ago."

Auntie Madeleine hadn't told her any of this.

"So, we're cousins, like, legally?"

"Oh! Well . . . I'm not sure. Kokum says that if someone in the family has died—like an aunt, uncle, grandmother, sister, or someone like that—you have to fill that hole with someone else; otherwise, it's like a piece is missing. It's the

Indian way. It's the way that you keep families strong. Oh, and Indian people are forever adopting people and—"

Misko cut her off. "Do you begin every sentence with 'oh' and always talk so fast?"

"Oh!" Shoshana clapped a hand over her mouth. "No. Well . . . probably," she mumbled.

She looked so chastised that Misko felt mean but she continued anyway. "So your Dad's white? Where's he from?"

"Kenora. I got his green eyes and light skin."

Now seated on the sofa, Misko glanced at Shoshana's pale skin and then looked down at her own brown hands. She flipped her hands over on her thighs and looked down at her palms. *Why can't the rest of my skin be this white? Why can't I have pale skin and green eyes?* Her shame feasted on. *Why do I have to have straight black hair? Why do I have to look so "Indian"?* She remembered slathering Noxzema on her face every night before bed, hoping that once it was washed off, she'd have nice white skin. But it didn't change her skin color one bit, except for an unsightly white blotch from overuse.

Her memory went even further back to the last time that she was here on the rez, when she was just six years old. When she and an older cousin were playing on top of an icy snowbank, the cousin had turned to Misko and said, "You could never be Snow Queen because you look too Indian. Don't you know you have to be either white or pale-skinned to win?"

Misko had stopped playing instantly. On the verge of making her acceptance speech, she threw down her stick microphone, slid down the icy snowbank, and ran all the way back to Kokum's. She went into the house and stared at her reflection in the mirror. She looked at her straight black hair, her dark skin, the dark this and the dark that, and then she ran outside and kept running until she was tired. She had heaved her little body on the frozen ground, pleading with God: *Why did you make me Indian? Why did you make me so ugly? Why did you make me this way? Why me?*

The bad memories evaporated as she looked up from her hands on her lap and came back to the present moment. Shoshana was sitting comfortably on the sofa like she belonged in *her* grandmother's living room. Like it was *her* place. Misko's eyes narrowed at the intruder as she finally interrupted her chattering. "I really don't know why you're here to sleep. What do you want, anyway?"

"Oh, I . . . I don't want anything. Honest. It's just that Kokum is sometimes afraid at night. She's afraid to be alone at her age . . . She has bad dreams and wakes up. So, I night-sit her. Like babysitting but at night."

"So what do you do exactly?" Misko continued her interrogation.

"I don't have to do anything. I just sleep on the sofa so she isn't alone. I try to help her. I've even attached a string from her bedpost to a little chain on the light bulb in her room. This way, Kokum can pull on the string and switch the light on or off while she's still in bed. I put it there to make it easier for her to see. Don't you think that was genius?" Shoshana smiled.

Misko softened a bit as she tried to imagine anyone doing that in Winnipeg. She couldn't picture Auntie Madeleine upsetting her apartment's sleek decor with a string and a bare light bulb, even when Misko used to be awakened by strange dreams and was afraid to go back to sleep, afraid of the dark and the city outside. "So your being here is a custom or something?"

"Oh! Oops! I mean, some people send their eldest child to live with their grandparents. Since I don't have grandparents, my mother sends me here. I've been coming for—"

"Do you get paid?" Misko interrupted.

"What? Paid? For helping someone? No, I don't get paid. Gee whiz."

Misko sensed she had reached a dividing line about the way their worlds worked. And this pale girl knew some of the rules of the rez better than she did. "Are you staying here tonight?"

Shoshana shook her head. "Well, you're here now. And I think my parents will be home later." She opened the door to go.

"How old are you, Shoshana?"

"Ten. I just finished grade five about a month ago. I wish school didn't stop for the summer. I like going every day. I got straight As in every subject. Someday, I want to go to university."

Misko watched Shoshana bounce down the steps and skip along the path. A feeling of envy rose up in her again. Shoshana seemed so chipper, so pretty, so smart, and so *white*. She wondered why she had to grow up with a busy auntie and a missing mom while Shoshana got to have both parents, even a father, and now *her* grandmother, too. It just wasn't fair.

Chapter Ten

———◆※◆———

The next morning, Misko brought tea to her grandmother—made the way she liked it. "Shoshana came
here last night. She didn't stay though."

"She's a good girl, that one," Kokum replied tenderly.

"Oh, did you want her to stay here, Kokum?"

"She can stay whenever she wants. She's family now."
Kokum nodded.

"How do you mean?"

"I'll show you with a picture. Get me a piece of paper
and something to write with."

Misko got up and went to get her notebook and crayons.
They were bunched altogether like a bouquet of stiff
flowers.

She followed Kokum to the table where her grand-mother tore out a piece of paper and picked out a red crayon. "Red's my favorite color," she said with her familiar grin. She then drew one big circle and said, "This is family." Then, she drew seven smaller circles along the big circle's inner edge so that all of them were connected to one another. "This circle here is your mom, this one here is your auntie, this circle here is me, this one's your cousin, and so on all the way around. You see how it starts here and ends with those we love. Everything's round, m'girl."

She then crossed out one circle and then another. "When people pass into spirit, die, or something happens to them, there is now a hole in the family. Like . . ." Her voice trailed off. She picked up the crayon again and traced back to a crossed-out circle one more time. "But now you have to put someone in that place to fill that hole in the family. Do you see, Misko? All these circles need to stay joined, connected."

"You mean replaced?"

"You can't replace people. But you can take people in, adopt them, make them your friend, make them your sister or your brother. Everyone becomes your family. That's love, m'girl, and that's what we Anishinaabe do." Kokum's voice was reassuring.

Misko stood up to get a better vantage point of the drawing of a circle made out of smaller circles. She stretched out her arm and imagined it on her wrist. "This looks sort of like a bracelet." She held up her wrist with the imaginary bracelet to show Kokum. "It's like a *family* bracelet."

"Heehee, that's right, m'girl, like a family bracelet!" Kokum beamed.

Misko thought about the bracelet from her dream, the one with the missing gem. *Where is that missing gem? What does it even mean?*

"Did my mother wear bracelets?" Misko asked. But when there was no answer, she exhaled her own impatience once again.

Chapter Eleven

In the morning, Misko got dressed, put her hair in a low ponytail, and went outside. She was halfway up the hill when she saw him again—the blond boy. Finally. He was in a fenced-off area watching another horse graze.

"Hey! Hey you!" she called. "I saw your horse the other day. He came right up to me and let me touch him. He's not afraid of me."

He ignored her.

"I said—"

"I heard you. And I don't care. You're not the one taking care of *breaking* him."

Horrible boy. Misko searched for something else to say, something hurtful and cutting, except . . . she wanted to know more about Mishtadim.

"Where did you get him?"

He looked her up and down and didn't say anything.

"Fine. Don't answer," she huffed, crossing her arms tightly over her chest.

"Fine, so I *will*," he said gruffly, leaning against the fence with his back to her. "My daddy buys horses from Alberta. Trains them up, rents them out. Or sells them."

"So why can't you train Mishtadim?"

"Who's Mishtadim?"

"The horse. That's his name, Mishtadim."

"That's a silly name for a horse. You're as crazy as your grandmother. His name's Brutus because he's one bad egg."

"Brutus? *That's a silly name*," she imitated in a high voice. "It's a terrible name, actually. No wonder you can't make him do anything. He has to act tough and mean to live up to a name like that."

"Do you know *anything* about horses?" the boy said with a sneer. "Or you just spouting off your mouth?"

"All I know is the horse came right up to me without having to call him. He likes *me*. So, I guess I know a thing or two about him."

"Look, my daddy's been raising and breaking horses all his life. And his daddy before him. And we're going to keep doing that right here," he snarled as he motioned to the ground with a karate chop. His hands then balled into fists as he straightened, looking at Misko. "So, I guess I know a thing or two about horses. Okay?"

She opened her mouth to argue but sensed the truth of what he said. What *did* she know about horses? *Well, my mother had a pony before I was born and I rode a pony five times at the winter carnival.* Instinctively, she knew to switch it up. "What's your name?"

"Why? You gonna change that, too?"

Without wanting to—it was the last thing she wanted to do but couldn't help herself—Misko giggled.

He cracked his knuckles. "I'm Thomas. After my granddad. I'm supposed to be his namesake, but . . ."

"But what?"

"But if you ask my dad," he said with an eye roll, "I'm a sorry excuse for a son. Not tough like my granddad. Guess I didn't get that tough gene. What's your name?"

"Miskobimizh."

"Whaa . . . Misk . . . What kind of name is that?"

"It's Anishinaabe and it means 'red willow.'"

"Anish-in . . . ?" Thomas fumbled over the word. "Don't you have a shorter name to describe who you are?"

"Yeah, Ani-shin-aabe," she repeated sarcastically, breaking up the syllables into bite-sized pieces for him to digest. "In case you don't know, that means 'Ojibway.'"

"Yeah, I heard of Ojibway before. So, your name means willow? You mean like a tree?"

"Yeah, like a red willow. Not the weeping kind," she clarified, waving her arms in the wind like tree branches, and then giggled.

"That's not a real name."

"But Lily is? Violet? Daisy? Jasmine? Flowers are okay? How 'bout stinkweed?"

He laughed so hard that his lips pulled back wide and his cheeks pushed up against his eyes.

"But you can call me Misko; everyone does."

"Misko," he said, his voice kinder, softer now. He repeated it: "Misko."

"That's my name, don't wear it out," she said playfully. She decided she might be able to like Thomas. Tolerate him, at least. "I got here . . . I mean, I got there," she corrected herself, pointing past the fence, "a few days ago from Winnipeg. I lived on the reserve until I was six and then we moved to Winnipeg."

"How come you moved?" he asked. "You know, I've *never* been on that side of the fence before."

Misko furrowed her brow and looked into his eyes to try to see what was going on behind them. He looked honestly curious, so she went on. "My mom left when I was four. I stayed for a couple of years, and then my aunt Madeleine took me to Winnipeg to live with her. To get a good education."

"Why didn't your aunt come here to live?"

"Her job is in the city. She's more of a city slicker, I guess. She likes shopping and restaurants. Loves Starbucks. She's what you'd call a businesswoman, I suppose."

"I've got an uncle in the 'Peg just like that, but I've never been. Maybe one day I'll go." Thomas squinted into the sun. "Why'd she go? Your mom?"

She shrugged. "Don't know." She felt her jaw clenching. "Look here, Sparky, you say that you've lived here most of your life and know a lot about horses, but why can't you train Mishtadim? If you're such a so-called horse expert, that is?" She was teasing him in that rough-and-tumble rez way. But her words had the opposite effect of their intent. She watched Thomas's eyes narrow and darken and wished she could take it back. She'd forgotten that white kids didn't know how to be kidded like her friends and family on the rez.

"Oh, I know what I'm doing. Don't you worry about that." Thomas glared at her with his hands squarely on his hips.

"Ah, you can take your hands off your hips. I didn't mean to make you mad. I was just teasing," she tried to explain.

"Well, I'm *not* joking. Like I said, Brutus is a bad, bad horse. As my dad likes to say, he's a bad *hoss*. Maybe it's not his fault . . . but he's still wild. His mom was taken away from him when he just a little foal."

"You mean he doesn't have a mother?"

"Nah. He never got properly bonded with his mare mom. People neither. Doesn't like to be handled and he doesn't trust anyone. Not me and not the other horses, neither."

"How old is he?"

"Maybe two and a half years old. So he's supposed to be used to us by now. You know, stuff like . . . let us groom him, check his hooves, and get a halter on him. But he won't let us. And if he doesn't soon . . ."

"What . . . what will happen if he doesn't?"

"We'll have to get rid of him. One way or 'nother."

"You mean sell him?"

"Maybe. But that would be bad for my daddy's batting average with horses. Can't have that now, can we? After all, what would the neighbors think?" Thomas finished in a voice drenched in sarcasm.

"Then what?" What's the other choice?" she demanded.

"You're just a dumb city girl, aren't you? What do you think the other choice is? First-class train ticket back to what my dad calls 'Le Foothills'?" He spat on the ground like his dad for added effect.

Misko's mouth went dry and she felt a pang of dread in her chest. "He'd kill him, you mean?" She could hardly say the words. "Your dad would kill a beautiful horse like Mishtadim 'cause he won't behave like he wants him to?"

"We don't say 'kill,' for your information. We say 'put down.'" Thomas looked indignant.

"Well, that's just a fancy word for murder . . . or for slaughter, isn't it?" she shouted, balling her hands into tight fists.

"Look, we're just trying to break him for his own good."

For his own good? Something cold circled her heart and then rose up and clicked in her mind. "You know what?"

"What?" he said, still looking annoyed.

"You tear him away from his mother and his home and then expect him to be 'good.' On top of that, you give him an awful name and force him to behave how *you* want him to. Maybe he doesn't want to be broken. Maybe he just misses his mom; ever think of that?"

"Like I said, we're trying to break him for his—"

"For his *own* good, yeah, you said that already. That's your answer for everything, isn't it? Break this and break that. Break down, break horses. Break, break, break . . . What's next, me?"

"What are you talking about?" He grabbed her arm and then let go when he saw her eyes narrow.

"I'm talking about kids our age or younger being broken. You know, ripped away from their homes, their moms and dads, brothers and sisters."

"What do you mean? Who was ripped away?"

"I'm talking about Native kids who were scooped up and taken away."

"Scooped up?"

"Yeah, scooped up as in *stolen* from their home and torn from every scrap of family they knew. My auntie said that the RCMP herded truckloads of kids to residential schools all over the country by trains, buses, trucks, you name it. Those kids sure weren't taken to nice boarding schools either."

"But why would they take them to those schools?" asked Thomas in disbelief.

"Because those schools were *designed* to break Indigenous kids. My auntie says that the schools were set up by the government and run by churches 'to kill the Indian in the child.' It was a way to turn us all into white people and to strip away our culture and take our land." She felt her face growing hot. "My auntie said that residential schools are the only schools in North America to have cemeteries built right next door." Misko sensed that he didn't believe her. Her eyes flashed, turning on him. "But you wouldn't know anything about this, would you?"

Thomas stared at her. "You're nuts." But he wasn't shouting. "People don't break children. Just animals."

"They were *treated* like animals," she shot back. "Beaten like animals, their hair shaved off like animals. And it was way worse for kids who tried to run away or broke the rules."

"What are you talking about?"

"I'm talking about how Native kids were punished for running away from those schools. Kids were whipped with a big leather strap, or locked in a closet, or thrown down the stairs, or put down in the boiler room for days or even weeks, and some kids even froze to death along the railway tracks. All of those kids were just trying to go home. What I'm saying is . . . is that it was almost impossible *not* to be broken."

Misko was so livid she started to shake.

"Are you okay?" Thomas's voice was quiet and soft. He was looking at her with wide eyes.

"What a question! Am I *okay*? Of course I'm not okay!" she screamed.

"Wow, that really was not what I was expecting."

"Really? What were you expecting, Disney?"

"I'm not sure but definitely not that."

"My mom's cousin, my uncle Ziibi, tried to run away from one of those residential schools. My auntie told me a bit about him. He was like a brother to her. Anyway, he just wanted to go home. You know how they punished him?"

Thomas just shook his head. He looked frightened— but curious.

"Those priests dragged him back to school and slammed his head into a radiator, face-first. That was his punishment for running away. That's how he lost his front teeth."

She saw Thomas's face go pale. Finally, he was starting to believe her.

"That's why Uncle Ziibi liked watching movie stars on TV so much, stars like Tom Cruise. You know that actor with the big white teeth? My uncle always wanted nice teeth like that, but instead he had to wear dentures for the rest of his life. Some kids *never* made it back home ever again, and some parents never found out what happened to their kids or where their kids were buried. Their graves are unmarked. But what would you know about it? Living here on this big ol' ranch with your daddy and mommy and grandpappy. Brothers and sisters, too, I bet. One big happy *Little House on the Prairie* family. What would you know?"

"You shut your mouth!" Thomas snapped.

"Go ahead, make me."

"Yeah, I'll make you."

She saw his fists clench and wondered if he'd do it. Hit her. She instinctively put a hand to her face, feeling for that sting that was the catalyst for her being here in the first place. She wanted the boy to make the first move. She dared him. This time she would fight tooth and nail. She wanted to get rid of whatever was clawing at her insides. But she stepped back—some other part of her knew that it wasn't right. This felt wrong.

"Don't worry. I'd never hit a girl. Even a dumb girl like you. You think you're so smart. Little Miss Know-It-All. For your information, I live here with just my dad. And I help him, I do. I help him work the ranch. He needs me to train the horses. And I don't care what you think!" His voice rose until he was shouting and his face looked hot with rage. "You hear me? My dad needs me! He needs me!"

"I never said anything about needing—" But by that time, Misko was talking to herself. Thomas was gone, awkwardly running down the hill along his side of the fence, stomping his anger into the ground. It was as if that was the only way he knew how to move across land.

Chapter Twelve

———✳———

Someday, Misko would like to beat Thomas in a race and show him what a girl could do. She could run rings around him. But he was mad at her. She felt a bit out of sorts despite the fact that she didn't even *like* that white boy. She didn't know what to do with herself, so she went to the one-stop grocery store and sauntered up and down the few aisles. She picked up a few items and then spotted Mr. Turner at the cash register and made a beeline for him. While he was busy with other customers, she waited near the register, flipping through the latest *Tiger Beat* magazine. Once the customers were gone, Mr. Turner motioned for her to come closer.

He handed her a stick of gum. "I remember you. You were just a little gaffer the last time I saw you," he said, smiling. "You still love horses?"

"Yes, I do!"

"Do you know what the most fascinating thing about a horse is?"

"What?"

"A horse can actually hear your heartbeat from four feet away."

"That's amazing!"

"Yesiree, sure is. They know what you're feeling and can sense everything. Your aunt Maddy was pretty good with horses when she was younger. How's she doing these days? She was always so busy." He paused thoughtfully. "Such a bright girl and a natural leader, too."

It was hard to think of her auntie as a girl, but Misko supposed she had been one *once*.

"She was your grandfather's favorite. After your mother, of course," he added, his eyes crinkling mischievously. "No, I'm just kidding. He loved them equally. But your grandfather did once get your mother a pony."

"I know! I saw a picture of them at Kokum's house."

"Yesiree, it was a hackney pony. He couldn't keep it where you currently live, so I let the pony live here with the rest." Mr. Turner waved his hand to indicate the grassy lot behind his store. In her mind, Misko saw four old ponies grazing back there, their bodies worn and soft as if widened by too many people taking rides.

"Do you have any horses now?" she asked.

His eyes clouded for a moment. He frowned and let out a sigh. "No. Sometimes it's about finding the right horse. Besides, I'm too old to look after them now, with the store and all . . . but I sure miss those horses. I even had a few mules to keep the coyotes away from the horses. Anyway, all of this grown-up talk must be boring you. Let me tell you about the fish fry! Everyone is going to be there, and our local group, the Lemon Sisters, are going to sing. They're a bit of an attraction 'round here." He perked up and Misko smiled at him encouragingly. He paused for a moment. "I suppose they call themselves the Lemon Sisters because they tend to hit a few sour notes here and there." He laughed mischievously.

He didn't seem mean at all, not like the other kids seemed to think. It was true he frowned sometimes, his mouth looking like an upside-down horseshoe, but he smiled, too. *People just see what they want to.*

When she got home, Kokum wasn't in the garden. Misko found her sitting in front of the TV watching a baseball game.

"Kokum, I got some things at the store. I'll make macaroni and cheese for supper. I saw Mr. Turner and he told me about the fish fry—"

"Shh, my dear. Come sit here," Kokum said, patting the seat beside her.

"Oh. Sorry, Kokum," Misko said, sitting down beside her.

"Watch . . . on third base. He's gonna steal home. You watch."

So Misko watched for the next half hour, knowing little about baseball, but happy to be sitting beside an energized Kokum. Misko wondered why she had never tried out for the school baseball team even though everyone said she was a natural athlete. Right now, she watched her grandmother talking to the TV set as if it was a real person: "Swing, batter, batter, swing! Oh, two out, 3–3, and bottom of the seventh inning. Oh oh, here comes that good batter now. He's a bit chubby, don't you think?"

Crack!

The batter hit the ball hard, sending it far into left field.

"Look at him run around the bases. Christopher Columbus! Can he ever run!"

When the game was over, Kokum said, "My team's going to win this year."

"I didn't know you liked baseball, Kokum."

"Ah-hey, and hockey and curling, too. I want to see Canada beat the U.S. team at the Olympics this year and I want whatchamacallit, what's his name again, Sid . . . Sidney Crosby to score the winning goal. Sid, I call him for short. Ayeee! Number 87."

"I didn't know that you like sports so much, Kokum."

"Ah-hey. Did you know that we had one of the best baseball teams around here? Howah, you should've seen your grandfather play ball. He was a switch-hitter. That means he could bat on both sides of the home plate. When he pitched, he put a lot of stuff on the ball. Could he ever make that ball curve!" Like a slow-motion replay, Kokum stepped up to an imaginary pitcher's mound, looked around, and then mimicked a ball gradually curving just ouside of the batter's box. "Stiii-riike," she continued enthusiastically. "He struck everybody out. One, two, three. One time, a batter finally got a hit and the ball went straight at your grandfather's head. It was coming so fast. He didn't even have time to put out his glove to catch it. He just caught it with his bare hand! By the cracky, those were the days! Did I tell you Noodin was even scouted by the New York Yankees?"

Noodin! She remembered that name from somewhere but couldn't quite match it to the name in red ink under the school photo. It was the name from her dream, too. Was he the man in the canoe who delivered her to the shore? He couldn't be ... "Noodin?"

"Ah-hey, your grandfather."

"*My* grandfather?"

"Yes. Mishoomis, that's how you say grandfather." Kokum nodded.

"Mr. Turner asked me about Auntie Madeleine. And he mentioned my grandfather, too."

"Ah-hey, that's right, m'girl. Your mishoomis and Willis Turner were good friends since they were boys."

Kokum walked over to the photos and passed Misko a framed one of a young couple sitting together at a community dance hall. "Me and Noodie. That boy sure could dance."

Misko felt a cold shiver run down her arms but didn't know why. "What happened to him?" she asked, but her grandmother grew silent and didn't respond. *Why doesn't anyone want to talk to kids about the things that really matter?* Misko wondered. Even Auntie Madeleine would get too upset to finish telling the story of her father. *And why doesn't anyone want to tell me what really happened to my mother?*

Later on in bed, Misko tossed and turned and kicked at her sheets, restless and wanting to be up and doing something that wasn't sleeping. *Sleeping can be so boring sometimes.*

She peeked around the towel she'd tacked over her window when she couldn't hang the blind back up. Through the haze of clouds hung a quarter moon. Misko felt a tingling in her toes and a lightness in her body, and she suddenly and achingly longed to be outside.

Could she? Kokum was asleep, so she tugged on her runners and stepped out the front door and slip-skidded her way over the stubble of weeds and last year's pine needles and moss. She hitched up her nightgown and scrambled over the fence and ran to where mist hovered on the hill.

The closer she got, the less she could see the mist, feeling only the dampness on her skin. And when she looked up, the moonlight shimmered. She remembered someone telling her the moon was called Nokomis Giizis. "Hello, Grandmother Moon," she said.

Misko looked down and saw the moonlight on her arms. It was the first time that she'd ever really seen this kind of light shining so beautifully on her skin. She felt the familiar wave of that otherworldly feeling where her body tingled, and then time expanded and collapsed on itself. Misko shook her hair loose from its braid. She stretched out her arms and twirled around and around. The past became the present and she could see herself as if from the sky, and she was there holding on to her mother's wrists—wrists that she could now see were covered in rivulets of raised, scarred skin in between bracelets of silver, turquoise, and leather.

She kneeled on the ground and pressed her face into the earth, smelling its damp richness, listening for its heartbeat. She held her breath and heard the sound of a dull thumping that sounded more like a horse's hooves moving over the earth.

Mishtadim! she thought. She rose to her feet. He was here! Somewhere close. She could sense him, and she strained to see. A cloud slid off the moon, and Mishtadim stood in its glimmer, whinnying, bobbing his head, and stomping at the ground. He was so perfect! An ache of longing swelled in her chest, a longing for something so magnificent and wild, as a muddled memory rose up in her that she couldn't quite place. Mishtadim watched her, not moving, until he turned suddenly, biting at something on his back.

And now she heard a distant buzz getting louder and louder, and she slapped at the swarm of mosquitoes. Mishtadim snorted and fled, and she did the same, her nightgown clinging to her legs. She climbed over the fence, rounded the corner of the house, and was up the steps before she heard a noise coming from the crawlspace underneath.

"Hello?"

Someone was hiding behind the large rain barrel.

"Who's there?"

Shoshana was hugging her knees, rocking back and forth. She lifted her face and it shone in the moonlight, wet from tears.

Chapter Thirteen

———✳———

Misko tugged Shoshana inside the house. "What happened?" she whispered, not wanting to wake Kokum.

For once, Shoshana spoke slowly, her words spaced apart, and not a waterfall of words. "Sometimes, when my daddy is away, my mom works night shifts and I'm alone and . . ." Tears slipped from her eyes. "And . . . I get scared."

"*You're* scared? I thought it was my grandmother who was scared."

"She is. But Kokum doesn't know I'm scared, too." Shoshana wiped her nose on her sleeve.

"And I've taken your place?" Misko asked.

"Oh! No! This is your place."

"But you came back tonight?"

"I couldn't sleep." Shoshana shrugged. "I don't have any brothers or sisters. I'm an only child, so it's just me at home. Sometimes, I'm afraid to be alone. I know I'm being a big baby, but am I supposed to be alone so much? I . . . I heard a big scary noise in the house. I . . . I didn't know what it was, so I ran here."

"Everyone gets scared sometimes, Shoshana. There's nothing to be afraid of. You could have just come in, you know."

Shoshana lowered her head. "This isn't your problem."

For a moment, Misko didn't know what to say. And then she thought, *What would Auntie Madeleine do?* "Now you listen to me." Misko stood, hands on her hips, imitating her aunt in gestures and words. "You are going to sleep here every night that you want to. You're my cousin. Right?"

Shoshana looked up at her, rubbing one eye. "Right, I'm your cuz."

"Now, where do you sleep? On this sofa, here?" Misko asked, pointing to where they were already seated. She pulled up the blanket over Shoshana, who was already curled up but still sniffling. "So-fa so good"? Misko asked gently. Shoshana smiled a little smile at the joke. Her eyelids were already starting to close and her forehead relaxed into the first waves of sleep.

"You don't have to feel alone now," Misko said softly; she gently stroked the girl's wet cheek. Shoshana smiled slightly and sighed, and a sense of protectiveness welled up in Misko. She was just a child after all. Misko remembered the many times that she felt afraid to be home alone. One time, she had almost burned the place down. That kind of thing happened when Auntie Madeleine took on extra hours. Misko had been trying to cook for herself when her sleeve caught on fire. The burn left a little scar on her forearm.

She had always wished that she had somewhere to go on those nights alone. She felt happy that Shoshana did have somewhere to go and that she could protect her.

Misko watched her drift off to sleep. She looked so peaceful and Misko wondered, *Does Shoshana have the same kind of dreams that I do? The kind that slip into another time? Like an old, deep time. Is this a direct line to my ancestors? Like the lines in the woodland painting that connect one world to another?*

Finally, Misko herself fell asleep and dreamed.

The northern lights come down to earth and they bring a beautiful woman back up with them. The northern lights don't speak words but communicate through sounds like static, crackles, and claps. The northern light beings give the beautiful woman a song and then return her back to earth. The gifted song has a special tone and a gentle sha sha sha shta shta sound that swirls in the hearts of the listeners. Its healing vibration calms a listener's spirit, mind, and body. The beautiful woman resembles her mother and sings her song on a horse, a cloud horse, cream and bone, decorated with refracted light.

Misko wasn't quite sure if the woman in the dream was her mother or what the dream meant. But for once she woke up feeling rested and strong and, this time, not at all haunted by her visions.

Chapter Fourteen

———◆※◆———

Shoshana was gone when Misko came into the kitchen the next morning. Kokum was always an early riser and was already sitting at the kitchen table with fruit, toast, and a ceramic mug of tea on the table in front of her.

"Did Shoshana get your breakfast?"

"Ah-hey."

"Is she gone already?" Misko asked and looked at the clock. It was only eight, but Shoshana had made time to help Kokum out of bed, make her breakfast, and even comb her hair into a silvery bun. Misko thought with a pang, *Why didn't I do that?* And then she remembered. *Kokum adopted her. She's her granddaughter, too. And I helped Shoshana. Everyone is needed and everyone has a place in the family.*

"That was good of Shoshana to help you this morning," Misko commented. "Auntie Madeleine would say that she has a good head on her shoulders."

"On her shoulders?" Kokum replied with a chuckle. "Where else is her head gonna be?" She chuckled some more.

Misko spread peanut butter and blueberry jam on toast and asked her grandmother if there was anything else she needed. "Over there," she said, pointing with her lips to the jar of withered daisies Misko had picked a few days earlier. "Anna liked daisies, too."

Straightaway, Misko was absurdly happy to have another connection, however small, with her mother. "She did? I'll go pick some fresh ones!"

After she ate, she tidied up the dishes and went outside eagerly, this time skipping along the fence down the hill. The fence was made of weathered logs that crisscrossed each other. She could see ax marks on the different-sized logs. They weren't machine-made. She saw some words carved on one of the fence posts and stopped to read them.

They were names of people, some she knew and some she'd only heard of. One thing that she did know was that they were all related to her: Ziibi, Chun, Flora, and Laura. They were all *supposed* to be cared for at residential school. And there was Noodin. Now she knew he was her grandfather, but what was meant by "Cree girl—three years old"? And finally, who had carved these names anyway?

Misko now walked back up the hill, counting 30 fence posts along the way before she saw the barn. It was an old building that had seen better days. Years of rain, sleet, and snow had taken its toll, and its scarlet red paint had been sun-bleached to a dull rust. In a fenced-off circle were two horses, and she could see Thomas but not Mishtadim. She didn't see any trucks or cars in the yard; hopefully, his dad wasn't around.

She watched Thomas intently for a minute, trying to determine his mood. He was raking the ground slowly, not banging his displeasure into the earth like last time. Maybe he'd be okay to talk to today? When Thomas looked up, she waved.

He ignored her, but Misko didn't care. She climbed over the fence and went to the enclosure. "Hi."

"You're on my property again."

"So?"

"So you're on my property. We own this land."

"You *own* the land? My Kokum says that there's no such thing as *owning* land."

"Whatcha mean? My granddaddy bought this place— paid for it with his own money. It's ours."

"You probably also think that those trees over there belong to you, huh?"

"If they're on our property, we own them," he responded irritably.

"What about the air, you own that, too?"

"Yep."

"That's the dumbest thing I ever heard. How can you own the air? You probably think that you own Mishtadim, too, huh?"

"Yeah, you know we do, matter of fact."

"Oh gawd." She rolled her eyes back in slow motion. "Why do humans get to *own* everything?"

"Ah . . . because we're smarter and better than all of the other animals put together," Thomas said unemotionally.

"But we're not. Humans aren't better and we're not at the top. Kokum says humans need animals to survive, but they don't need us. We need plants to survive, but they don't need us. They all could live without us, but we can't live without them. Ever think of that?"

"Look, I'm working here. I don't have time to talk about who's at the top of the food chain or argue with you whenever you have nothing better to do."

"Why are you raking all that dirt anyway?" she asked.

"Makes it easier for the horses. For their groundwork."

"What do you mean?"

"It means teaching them good manners on the ground. Before you get into the saddle."

"Manners? For a horse?"

"I was right. You really don't know much. That's right, city girl, *manners*," he said loudly as if she were hard of hearing. "Like not letting the horse misbehave or get in my way or push me around. I'm the one who decides which direction to go. They have to know who's boss."

"Maybe he doesn't like being pushed around all the time," she countered. "Maybe you have to give him some say."

"Some say? That's goofy. Who ever heard of a horse having a say? Sheesh." Thomas snorted. "He has to listen to my commands and signals and that's that."

"Maybe *you're* the one who needs to listen! Ever think of that?"

"Nope."

"Ever think what would happen if you were kind and patient with him instead of mean and rough?"

"Nope. And, for your information, I'm not being mean, it's the way—"

"You are, too!" Misko pointed to the other horses. "What are you going to do, beat these ones, too?"

His shoulders hunched and he stopped raking. "Nope. Don't have to. My dad likes these ones and never beats them. Their names are Star and Blaze."

Misko looked at the horses. "Which is which?"

"Are you kidding? You don't even know . . ." Thomas snickered. "Look at the markings on their forehead. One horse has a star and the other horse has a blaze, a long white stripe down the middle of his face. Get it?"

Misko wanted to mouth off but instead said, "Got it."
And when he smiled, she said, "Will you do groundwork
with Mishtadim?"

"Nope."

"Why not?"

"Because we don't have a horse by that name here."

"Aw! Don't be like that. Where is he?"

"In his stall. And I know what you're doing. You're
asking all kinds of questions and now I'm talking to you,
just like you wanted."

"I'm not stopping you from working. I just wanted to
talk."

"Listen, are you trying to find the longest way possible
to tell me what you came here for?"

"Can I help with the horses?" she blurted.

"Well . . . My dad's away. What you really want is to
see Brutus, right?"

His dad's away! "Oh! Could I?" She didn't correct
his name this time. She didn't want him to tell her to *get
lost.*

"Well, I guess I could show you around. Show you all
the work I have to do around here," Thomas said with a
sigh, unlocking the gate. "It's a man's job, you know."

Misko almost laughed, but she pursed her lips tight
together to keep from saying what was really on the tip
of her tongue. The hinges creaked as Thomas opened the

big barn doors. She followed him in. She'd never been in a barn before. It was the smell that hit her first. She waited for her eyes to adjust to the soft, filtered light. The smell was sweet and musty—a damp grass, dung-mixed loamy smell. "I thought manure would stink."

"Manure is just pooped-out grass and hay. But my dad makes me rake the stalls every day."

There were two rows of stalls, five on each side, and a loft that hung from the ceiling. She saw only four horses. "How come?"

Thomas looked at her as if she had two heads. "Would you want to stand in poop and piss all day long? And besides, it keeps down flies and parasites. Too expensive if a horse gets sick."

"I meant, how come your dad makes you do it?"

"I already told you. He needs me to mind the ranch when he's away. He counts on me. Like today. He's taken two horses to sell."

She felt dizzy. "Did he . . . did he take Mishtadim?"

Thomas pointed to the stall at the row's end, and she saw the familiar dark brown hindquarters of Mishtadim. She pulled two carrots out of her pocket.

"You didn't plan this at all, did you?"

"Maybe just a teensy-weensy bit," she said in a small voice.

Misko walked past the first three horses, which lifted their heads, swiveled their ears, and sniffed the air. She hid her hand behind her back, wishing she'd brought the whole bunch of carrots.

The horse closest to Mishtadim didn't move at all when she went by. The mare looked scraggly with uneven ears; she didn't even lift her head, sniff, or stomp. Misko could see that the mare's eyes were dull. "Oh! She looks . . . so sad." She turned to Thomas. "There's no light in her eyes. How come?"

"Shut-down. That's what they call it. She doesn't respond to the whip or spurs or being led by the halter. Just gave up—some horses do." Thomas cleared his throat. "She's next to go. Can't waste money on a shut-down."

"You mean, she just shut down . . . like her emotions and stuff?"

"That's right."

"What do you mean she has to go?" Misko asked.

"We're going to see if we can sell her."

Misko tried to give her one of the carrots, but the mare didn't respond at all. Not even a sniff. She felt a tug in her heart for the horse but forced herself to keep moving down the stalls.

"Mishtadim!" she called. "Mishtadim . . . it's Miskobimizh. Look what I've—" She tugged at the door that was stuck and it flew open and smacked the rail. She went into his stall and saw his hindquarters facing the gate. Frightened by the sound, Mishtadim lifted his leg high to his side, folded his knee back, and then kicked sideways. The blow was quick and sharp, and the shock was great. The pain exploded in her chest as she stumbled backward a few steps and fell. She heard a whinny and Thomas shouting, "Roll! Roll away!"

She could hear Thomas's voice and moved out of the way before the hoof came down again. Scrambling back on all fours, she felt Thomas behind her, his hands under her arms, tugging her away from Mishtadim's fury.

Chapter Fifteen

Misko couldn't breathe without it hurting. Her right shoulder and upper arm were throbbing, and her chest was aching. She was sure she was going to throw up or black out, or maybe both at once.

"Are you crazy?" Thomas was breathing heavily, his nostrils flaring. "Don't you know? You never—*ever*—walk up behind a horse. Not *any* horse. 'Specially not that one!"

She couldn't stop sobbing, great huge gulping sobs.

"Come on, Misko." Thomas's voice softened. He was now pulling her up to standing. "Let's get you inside and we'll have a look. It's probably nothing. I've been kicked loads of times." He talked on and on and Misko moved slowly with his arm around her.

He opened the kitchen door and rushed her inside to sit at the big wooden kitchen table. He helped her remove her top layer. "Ow, ow, ow," she repeated.

"Dang, that's messed up!" he said.

Misko looked down. At the edge of her tank top, spreading into her armpit, was a red welt about the size of a baseball.

"That's gonna be a real bad bruise." Thomas got up and fetched ice from the freezer. He wrapped the ice in a tea towel and pressed it against the swollen flesh of her upper arm and shoulder. "Nothing's broken as far as I can tell. Skin's not broken either. I've seen worse. I saw a man get kicked in the mouth once. That wasn't pretty. And I got kicked in the butt a few times."

Misko listened and knew Thomas was talking a lot to keep her conscious and to distract her from the pain. "But why?" she asked. "Why'd he do it?"

"You always have to be careful around a horse. Even a well-trained one. They're skittish. It's their heritage from thousands of years. Their . . ." Thomas scrunched up his nose. "It's the way that they've been hardwired. They've been attacked by wolves and lynx and cougars and everything that's looking for a meal. They're scared of the stupidest things; even a plastic bag stuck on a fence snapping in the wind spooks them."

"But Mishtadim liked me before. He let me touch him. He wasn't frightened then." She remembered now how he had fled when the grouse flew out of the brush.

"Well, I bet you didn't creep up on him from his ass side and yell his name like you were yelling 'Boo!'"

That made her laugh and then her nose ran. She put her arm up to wipe it and pain shot through her upper body. "Ow ow ow ow ow!"

"I know that it hurts, believe me, but that's nothing. Wanna see my scar?" he asked, trying to deflect her pain.

"Ow—okay."

"Look here on my leg. You see this big gash? I fell off a horse and landed right on a sharp rock. Twenty stitches," Thomas bragged, as if it was something to be proud of.

"Well, I got this scar on my arm here," she said, pointing to the inside of her forearm.

"Cool scar. It looks like a crescent moon," he remarked.

"It wasn't cool at all because I burned myself on a hot stove," she quipped.

"Ouch! Well, I have scar on my forehead, just here near my hairline. It's tiny, but if you look closely, you can see—"

"Naw, our little scars are nothing."

"What do you mean, Misko?"

"My mom went to one of those residential schools. On her wrists, she had scars. A teacher used to put her hands on the hot radiator whenever she spoke her own language."

"Whoa, no way."

"Yes way. But that didn't stop her. Auntie Madeleine said that she spoke Anishinaabemowin, that's the Ojibway language, to the other kids at recess when the nuns weren't looking. She whispered lullabies and little prayers in their tiny ears at night. My mom felt especially sad for the kids weeping at night because they just wanted to go home. They just wanted to see their moms and dads. One day, a nun caught my mom talking Anishinaabemowin to this new girl at recess. The girl was crying because she couldn't understand one word of English and my mom was just trying to help her. The nun slapped my mom across the face and warned her never to speak that 'savage' language again, and then she dragged her by the ear all the way to the principal's office where she got the strap."

"The strap! For a girl?" Thomas exclaimed.

"Yep, and not the black one—the *red* one. That one hurts the most and can leave a mark, even a scar!"

"Geez."

"Auntie Madeleine said that the teachers didn't even call my mom by her own name after that. She was just a number, like she wasn't a real human being or something. They wouldn't let other kids talk to her, sit with her, or even eat the same food as they did. Her clothes even had a number marked on them."

"I can't imagine not being called by my own name in school," Thomas mused out loud.

"My auntie said that giving my mom a number was a way of taking away her identity and making her feel ashamed of who she was. It was all part of breaking her down."

"Where's your mom now?"

"I imagine she's out there somewhere, still running. Kokum says that I got good strong legs like my mom," she said, pointing to her calf muscles. "My mom is probably leaping over big puddles and running through tall grass, jumping over huge rocks, and running wherever she wants to. I imagine her bracelets shining in the sun, deflecting anything that could harm her," Misko murmured dreamily, as Thomas watched her intently.

"She sounds like a bit of a superhero," he said softly.

"She is to me! Hey, you ever think that superheroes aren't just dreams or fantasies? I mean, we're so much more than what we can see. Maybe we do have special powers. Maybe we're just *remembering* where we originally come from?" she said, looking out the window up at the sky. When she turned back to Thomas, she could see what she'd said was buffering in his brain. *This might take a while*, she thought, so she changed the subject. "Where's *your* mom, Thomas? Isn't she here when your dad's away?"

Thomas's eyes narrowed. "Do you want a Coke?" he asked instead of answering.

He got a can and poured. Misko watched as he tilted the glass like a pro, so the foam came right to the rim without spilling over.

"Fancy pouring," she said.

"Yeah, but we're not fancy folk 'round here." He chuckled. "We don't even say grace before meals. It's just my dad and me, so we just say, 'On your mark, get set, go!' Hey, want some horsed ovaries to go with that there Coke?"

"Do you mean hors d'oeuvres?" Misko pronounced the word with a bit of flair.

"Duh, that's what I said." He winked. "My dad showed me how to pour like an expert. Except it was beer."

Misko took the Coke and her hand touched his. She recalled those same callused hands pulling her away from Mishtadim.

"Tink, tink," she said and gave a little smile as they clinked their glasses. She decided to tell the truth. "About my mom . . . I have a lot of question marks. I don't know where she is. She just disappeared. We lived with my grandmother when I was little, and one day she didn't come home. No one saw her again and she didn't write or call. But she used to run away sometimes when she was younger. So . . . we just don't know. I always hoped that not hearing from her all these years meant she just didn't want to be in touch, but now—" Misko shut her eyes tight to stop the tears. She focused on the pain radiating from her shoulder to distract herself. It hurt. A lot. *Good.*

Tsss kerr-pop. Thomas opened another can of Coke and gulped it down. "Ah, I'm sorry 'bout your mom. Guess I'm better off. My mom comes and goes," he said, wiping his mouth with his forearm. "We got family in Kenora and she stays there mostly. Her and my little brother."

"So, it's just you and your dad here and no one else?" she asked. Misko saw his jaw tighten and she waited.

"Yeah, just my dad and me . . . He does get mean sometimes though. Meaner when he's drunk, and really mean when he's falling down drunk. And then my mom can't cope and takes Billy away and leaves . . . leaves me here to— Look, my dad's had a hard life, you know. His dad was hard on him, beat him up pretty bad, so he gets mean when he drinks. My dad says that the world has teeth and it bites, so you'd better bite *first*. I know he's hard, but you got to understand that his heart's in the right place."

"Seems to me like it's in the wrong place. The way he treats—"

Thomas stood up. "I should get back to work now."

She followed him outside and spotted the barn. "Hey, can I go see Mishtadim? I don't want him to think I'm mad at him. It wasn't his fault."

"Suit yourself. Geez, you're as stubborn as a mule. Just remember to breathe, okay."

"Breathe?"

"Yeah, try to relax your breath. Take a big breath in and then exhale. Do it three times. Horses can pick up on someone being nervous around them."

They walked toward the barn and stood outside. She still felt the pain in her chest and was still scared to take a bigger, deeper breath. She looked away momentarily to concentrate on her breathing, and then she nodded at

Thomas, signaling that she was ready to go into the barn to see Mishtadim. She went in and found the two carrots in the hay where she had stashed them.

"Keep your hand open and flat," Thomas said. "Unless you want a horse bite today, too. And I don't mean a horse-fly bite, I mean a bite straight from the horse's mouth."

She could hear still him talking, but his words grew fainter the farther she went into the barn. She moved slowly inside, inhaling the warm scents of animals, adjusting again to the murky light. Barn swallows flitted above her, moving from nest to beam, twittering their call of *cheep, cheep, cheep* followed by a *churee* whistle. A mole slipped past her foot, looked up at her with his small dot eyes, and scampered off. Misko was unafraid.

She felt sheltered, enclosed, and protected from the outside somehow. The sounds from that world were muted and muffled. Out there—out there her mother *was* or . . . *wasn't*. Here, she knew exactly what to expect and that felt safe. She hummed softly; a familiar tune rose up and came to her out of nowhere. She moved near Mishtadim's stall and waited until he sensed her. Right hand outstretched and flat, she waited.

He watched her every move out of the corner of his eye. Enticed by the carrot, he sniffed the air, and she wondered if he could also smell her pain. He reached his head over the gate and nosed around for the carrot from her flat hand. He took it gingerly, his soft fleshy lips tickling her palm, and then she went cautiously into his stall.

"Good boy, Mishtadim," she whispered, and the horse turned his whole head and seemed to be listening attentively. "Beautiful Mishtadim. I'm sorry if I upset you." She offered the second carrot and a third and while he was chewing, she gave him a well-deserved scratch and patted his shoulder. He pushed his nose into her injured armpit and blew, as if healing her hurting. "I know you're scared, Mishtadim. We all get scared sometimes, but don't be afraid of me," she whispered. "I'm just like you. Your mother died and my mother . . . left, so I know how you feel. Just don't be scared. We'll figure it out. You and me. You'll see."

Mishtadim leaned his head into her, and she breathed in the wonderful horsiness of him.

When he bobbed his head up and down, she slowly backed out of the stall. As she passed by the shut-down mare, she felt a tug in her chest and a lump in her throat.

"Mishtadim and I are friends again," she announced, walking out of the barn.

Thomas was waiting outside. "Are you for real?" he asked, incredulous. "You're brave, I'll give you that much. I wouldn't go near a horse that tried to kill me."

"He didn't try to . . ." She saw he was kidding—maybe —and so she smiled. "Thanks, Thomas. For being nice."

Thomas blushed and turned away. "I'm putting Brutus

out to pasture tomorrow. If you want to talk to him again. Or whatever it is you think you're doing."

"That is if I live through the night," she teased back and waited until she saw him grin. She gave a little wave and turned around and walked down the hill. She was aware of the throbbing in her right arm and shoulder, but the joy in her heart leaped up and excited her even more.

Chapter Sixteen

She could smell bacon frying as she walked across the yard. Kokum and Shoshana were in the kitchen talking and didn't hear her come in. Misko stood in the doorway for a moment, watching how comfortable they were together. Her arm throbbed.

"Hi, Misko. We made supper," Shoshana said when she noticed her standing there.

"I thought you just came here to sleep?" Misko heard the edge in her own words, but Shoshana didn't notice.

"Oh! Well, my mom's working two shifts right now. When I saw Kokum in the store, I said we should make bannock for you 'cause you wouldn't have had it in Winnipeg. We used bacon fat instead of margarine so it's extra special and tasty."

"What made you think that I've never had bannock there? I've had it lots of times. Restaurants serve it there, you know?"

"Oh! Really? In restaurants? I didn't know."

Misko looked at the table. *Not how Auntie Madeleine taught me.* She saw that Shoshana had arranged the knives and forks differently and brought over the vase of daisies— the daisies *she'd* picked.

Shoshana carried the heavy cast-iron skillet to the table and served bacon and eggs.

"We're having breakfast for dinner?" Misko asked sarcastically.

Kokum looked at Misko with a quizzical expression on her face, and immediately Misko felt awful again for being so . . . *jealous. I have to stop.*

Then her grandmother pulled apart the bannock, gave Misko the first warm piece, and watched her bite through the crispy crust. "It's good you've come home, m'girl," Kokum said sweetly.

Misko blinked back tears, feeling silly and childish. "This is . . . yummy, way better than anything in the city."

"Oh good! Sometimes I even mix in blueberries or raisins," offered Shoshana.

There she goes again . . . I did this, I did that . . . She's exhausting, Misko thought.

"What's the city like?" Shoshana asked.

Misko told them about school and her friends there, and she described the Friendship Center she belonged to. And she even told them about David, a boy she liked. Kokum tsk-tsked and grinned. Misko didn't say anything about the reason Auntie Madeleine sent her here. She wanted the evening to remain as friendly as it was turning out to be. She didn't want to alarm anyone. She wasn't sure Kokum knew what happened or why she was here in the first place. She reached for a second piece of bannock and winced.

"What's wrong? I thought that you said it was delicious?" Shoshana asked.

"It is . . . My arm just hurts."

"Oh! What happened?" The younger girl's eyes went big, eyebrows raised, mouth turned down. She really was still such a child.

Misko told them about the horse called Brutus—but not about Thomas. *What if I'm not allowed to be in a barn on the other side of the fence?* "The horse was grazing by the fence and I startled him," she fibbed, taking off her sweatshirt to show them the bruise.

Shoshana gasped. "Oh, that looks pretty bad! You mean the fence by the ranch? Was that boy there?"

"Do you know him?"

"Yep, his name is Thomas and he's awfully cute. Lots of girls think so, but I heard that his dad's real mean so no one goes over there."

Kokum gently touched her bruise. "Poor girl," she said, lightly kissing it. "Gidimaagendagozi, all better now, m'girl?"

Misko nodded, feeling her grandmother's love. *Now that's real medicine. Mashkiki.*

Kokum murmured, "Anna had big bruises like that."

"Was she kicked by a horse, too?" Misko asked.

"Kicked." Kokum sighed, shaking her head. "Thrown. Bit. That Desjardins boy didn't know what the heck he was doing with them horses. Anna was just trying to help."

"Who's the Desjardins boy?" Misko asked.

"Which boy?" Shoshana said.

"I bet she means Thomas's dad," Misko guessed. She tried to imagine him as a young man even though it was hard. He was a strange blur of a much older Thomas, and he was the man who had tried to whip Mishtadim. She wondered if he used to be like his own son, all smirks and jokes, just waiting for the pretend tough-guy surface to be cracked open. She wondered what broke Thomas's father.

Kokum piped up, "I don't want you going near that ranch. I don't want you getting kicked or hurt like Anna."

Shoshana went to the bookshelf. "Oh! It's gone. I wanted to show you the picture of your mother, Anna, with her pony."

"I took it. It's in my room." Misko hurried to fetch it. "I'm sorry, Kokum. I should've asked."

"I think you look like her, Misko. So pretty." Shoshana smiled.

Misko dipped her head. No one had ever told her she was *so* pretty before. People had described her mom as beautiful or a whole lotta pretty in one place. They told Misko that she looked like her mother, but she doubted it. But after being here on the rez, she heard it often enough that she was starting to believe it. She changed the subject away from the compliment: "What was his name—the pony's name?" she asked.

"Mishtadim," Kokum answered.

Everything went silent. Time slowed. Misko knew Shoshana was talking, but her voice was muffled and seemed to come from far away. The picture frame slipped through her fingers and fell as if in slow motion.

"What a silly name for a horse," Shoshana was saying, catching the frame at the last moment, jolting Misko back to real time. "It means 'big dog' or technically 'big elk.' And that's what they used to call a horse. In the language, I mean. So, this pony was named Big Elk!"

Mishtadim. How could I know your name, out there on the hill? She shivered, remembering how the name had floated into her mind, whispered by an unseen voice.

Later on, after Kokum went to bed, Misko said to Shoshana, "That sofa is a bit lumpy. Do you want to sleep in my room? Pretend we're having a sleepover?" *What if she says no?*

But Shoshana said yes, and they spent a long time gabbing before they fell asleep. Shoshana wanted to know more about Winnipeg, and Misko asked her about Thomas's dad, Mr. Desjardins, as Shoshana called him.

Shoshana shrugged. "He's not a nice man. He's mean to Thomas. I don't really know much about him."

So Misko changed the topic, remembering how much the younger girl liked going to school. They both talked about the kids they knew on the rez, and who liked whom, and who were mortal enemies. Misko thought that even though being here on the rez felt different from city life, the girl talk was essentially the same.

She slept well that night, Shoshana's little snores lulling her off to dreamland.

Chapter Seventeen

The next day was rainy, and not city rain where you could still go out with an umbrella and stay dry darting under store awnings. This was pure country rain, pelting down hard from a granite gray sky, a sky not broken up into jigsaw pieces by tall buildings. It was the kind of rain that stung your face and swept your hair in all directions. And the fantastic boom, clap, and rumble of animikii, the thunder beings, was exhilarating.

Misko flipped through some paperbacks she found, well-thumbed and worn—*Black Beauty, National Velvet,* and *The Black Stallion.* She wondered if they were her mother's. She loved how books had adventures inside waiting to be discovered. Restless indoors, with the rain thundering on, she asked Kokum more questions than usual, but her grandmother only ever answered the ones she wanted to answer. The only other question Kokum answered today was about the names carved in the wooden fence, but after talking about that, she didn't answer any more questions.

That's the way it was in Anishinaabe culture, not as much talking as in white culture. *Elders say we have two eyes, two ears, and one mouth for a reason. One ear is for listening and the other one is for hearing. And respect means that before you start speaking, you listen to the other person first.* But Misko wanted answers right now and she had to breathe into her impatience again and again and exhale the hurry-up part of herself.

The rain let up around suppertime, filling Misko with hope that it wouldn't rain the following day. Everything smelled sweet, fresh, and alive. More birds chirped, more frogs croaked, and the bark of trees glistened. But sometime in the middle of the night, the rain had started up again. She was half asleep when she heard the pitter-patter of rain on the roof, *drip drop, drip drop, drip drop.* Snuggled and warm in her bed, Misko heard the rain's watery melody whisper and shush, and she felt surrounded by everything that ever was. When the rain started coming down harder, she felt the excitement as the staggered uproarious beats came down faster, as if she had climbed inside a big, tight drum.

In the morning, she walked to the fence to see Mishtadim, wondering if he was cranky, missing her as much as she missed him. She hoped Thomas was letting him graze on the hill as he had promised. She guessed the horse wouldn't venture as far as where she stood, the grass still wet and bright after the rain.

She heard a soft flutter of wings. She didn't move or turn her head and stood very still. Soon, one after the other, two gray jays landed on the fence beside her. Their heads were tilted, puzzling out who she might be, and they weren't afraid. Their feathers were all shades of charcoal—ash and smoke, silver and steel, salt and pepper—as if bred to blend into the fog and mist of the rain-soaked air. Their chirping and singing invigorated Misko's sense of hope and excitement. She thought that it would be nice to pick some daisies for Kokum. They seemed to spring up every-where after the rain.

Suddenly, she heard a roaring, sputtering noise; turning, she saw Nelson on his ATV.

"Hey, Misko!" he shouted. "Want to shoot hoops with us?"

"For sure," she shouted back and ran up to the ATV.

Misko rode with Nelson along the back trail under pine, poplar, tamarack, and the dripping cedars near the lake. They came to a birch tree leaning out over the water, a hoop attached to it, and a bunch of kids, both in and out of the water, were playing some zany version of b-ball.

"No rules! No teams!" Sage called. "You need to dunk in this game. Just get as soaking wet as you can. Get it? Dunk! Slam dunk! Woot woot!"

And soon Misko was as dripping wet as everyone else. She had no idea that she could laugh so much. The day went by so fast. Someone's mom brought packages of hot dogs and marshmallows, and Nimkii and Nelson lit a fire. Zach, a boy she didn't know, handed out long sticks and everyone roasted hot dogs over the coals.

Autumn, dry and dressed in a hoodie and leggings with a wet, thick braid snaking down her back, crouched beside Misko and elbowed her gently. "You okay?"

"Yeah, I'm good. That was so much fun."

"It's nice to have you here," Autumn said, her voice warm. Misko smiled nervously as her cousin was six years older and much more confident.

"Is it okay if I sit here?" she asked, and without waiting for an answer plunked herself down on the log beside Misko. "Maybe I'll see you in the 'Peg one of these days. It's a pretty cool city in a lot of ways." After a short break, Autumn said, "I'm going there next year. I want to take science at university because someday I want to be an astronomer. I love learning about science and our star stories," she said, gesturing to the sky.

"Oh, I would love that," Misko squealed.

Autumn looked up at the sky again. "You know, a certain darkness is needed to see the stars," she explained.

When she flung her long braid around by the light of the fire, Misko thought it looked like the tail of a comet.

Misko asked, "Are you gonna come back here to live after university?"

"Absolutely," Autumn replied. "I'm going to come home as much as I can, always. This is home."

"Yeah, you must love it here on the rez."

"It's not about the rez. That's just a government construct. I'm talking about the land, our homeland. N'Dakii Miinan. I was born and grew up here, and so was my mother, grandmother, great-grandmother, and so on down the line. Maybe it's through osmosis or something, but the spirit of the land gets inside you. It *never* leaves you. Maybe it's the ancestors in my blood memory who guide me, but I definitely know where I belong."

Misko's eyes welled up at her words. *Is this where I belong, too? Is this my home? What does home even mean? If Autumn comes home all the time, and Mishtadim is here, and my friends . . . and with Shoshana here, and Kokum, of course—it could be a possibility to live here on the rez. But I'd really miss my aunt, the track team, and the oodles of things to do in the city.*

"Of course, city people will say that moving back home after university means that I failed somehow," continued Autumn. "That I somehow couldn't make it in the city, and *had* to move back. But that won't be the case. The land calls you home." Misko felt flushed and a little uncomfortable under the older girl's unwavering wise stare. Still, she loved that Autumn spoke to her like a grown-up and not like a child. Autumn's eyes searched her face. "Hey, you know, things can get a bit rough in Winnipeg with all of the racism. Bad things do happen. But you're careful out there, right?"

"Sure, a-a-always," Misko replied nervously. She debated telling Autumn about the man who slapped her. But as soon as the negative thought crept into her mind, Misko's breath grew shallower, faster.

Autumn must've noticed something, because she reached out and briefly squeezed her hand. Misko looked down at their hands folded together and smiled. Autumn's hand was the same color as hers. Brown. And when she looked up, she noticed that Autumn's eyes were the same color as hers. Brown. She could see herself reflected in Autumn's gaze and felt so at home there.

"You know, people talk about the city being dangerous," said Autumn, "but I know it's all about how you . . . navigate it. It'll be good to have each other's back," she added with a wink. "You can show me around. Show me all the cool places," she finished, flicking her braid over her shoulder to the front.

Misko felt the tension leave her body. She suspected that somehow Autumn knew what had happened to her in Winnipeg, or maybe she had just heard that *something bad* happened? She was grateful that the older girl didn't press her but seemed to know exactly what to say.

She felt a bit at a loss for words. "You have beautiful hair," Misko blurted.

"Gee, thanks. It just feels good to have it off my face, especially when it's wet. Do you want me to braid your hair like mine? Come, ambe, sit here," Autumn said, motioning to the ground in front of her.

Misko scampered over and sat cross-legged on the ground. If she had a tail, it would be wagging.

Autumn gently touched the back of Misko's head with her hand. "You have nice hair, too. You have what we call Indian hair, thick and strong," she said, dividing Misko's hair into three sections and starting to braid strand over strand.

"My aunt usually braids my hair," Misko said. "She puts a prayer into it: manitou, nendamowin, wiiyiw."

"Spirit, mind, body," echoed Autumn. "That's the way we braid sweetgrass, too—wiingashk—the hair of Mother Earth. Here, can you hold the end so that I can braid it nice and even, like mine?" Misko complied.

"You see up there," Autumn said, motioning to the night sky with a free hand. "That cluster of stars over there is the Pleiades, called the Seven Sisters by some, but we call it Bagonegiizhig, the Hole in the Sky. It's where we come from."

"We came from up there?"

"Ah-hey. We came from up there and we'll go back up there. We Anishinaabe call ourselves the star people, after all."

"The star people," Misko repeated out loud.

"Yeah, we believe that there's 'the other side.' It's where we all come from. We come from Geezhigo-Kwe, Sky Woman, who fell through the hole in the sky into this world. Have you heard about her?"

Misko shook her head.

"Let's see, how can I describe this? A time long ago, the world was in darkness. Hey, ever notice how so many stories start like that? Anyway, back then, light only came from the other side. When Sky Woman fell through the hole, she created a path of light all the way down to earth. Imagine a maple seed twirling and whirling, falling all the way down to earth; that's what Sky Woman looked like as she fell through the hole in the sky. In her belly she brought life, and in her hands she brought seeds and branches of every kind from the Tree of Life on the other side."

"That's epic," Misko whispered.

"She must've looked like a tiny speck of dust falling in a shaft of dazzling light all the way down to earth." Autumn beamed, swaying her hand to illustrate.

"I so want to learn what you know."

"You can. Start right now. Put your arm out and reach for the stars," Autumn instructed Misko.

She didn't think twice before extending her arm toward the sky. It was incredible—it did feel as if she could touch them.

"You see, now you're that much closer to what you want, just by reaching for it." Autumn smiled. "An *arm's length* closer, in fact. Yep, all big things have small beginnings."

"There's so many stars up there," Misko said in awe. She extended her other arm effortlessly and cupped her hands together.

"That's dope. When you put your arms up like that, you look like you're holding up the stars. Like you're holding up our ancestors. Autumn smiled again. "Odoobina' anangoog, that's a perfect name for you: She Holds Up the Stars." Misko smiled widely and enjoyed the new discovery while Autumn busied herself with roasting herself a marshmallow.

Misko's mind raced, picturing the two of them making trips back and forth between the city and the rez, hanging out over Christmas and March Break. She pictured Autumn in the city cheering for her at track meets and going to cool places like art galleries and skateboard competitions. There was no shortage of things to do in the city. She pictured them on the rez, too, snowshoeing through bright, crisp snow, roasting hot dogs and marshmallows, and having long conversations about galaxies, nebulae, star clusters, and Sky Woman. After all, the stars were visible here . . . here at *home*. Misko's heart pounded with excitement. They would become friends . . . sisters even.

Maybe we could even exchange friendship bracelets. Misko giggled at the thought.

"What's so funny?" Autumn's eyes twinkled.

"Oh, nothing," Misko said, giving her a big smile.

"Okay, nichi. You can tell me later," Autumn said, as she began roasting another marshmallow.

It was getting late, and Misko was finally starting to feel tired. She got up and stretched, but it did nothing to lessen the hold of sleep, weighing down her shoulders and making her yawn.

"Okay, sleepyhead, it's time to go," Autumn said, turning to her. "We'll be here all summer. Well, Sage will be at least. I've got to go to the city for a few days."

"I hope that I'll see you around?" Misko said shyly.

"You bet you will," Autumn responded, her eyes serious and unwavering before she broke into her luminous smile.

Chapter Eighteen

———✳———

The next day, Misko walked briskly along the fence line downhill, her runners squelching on the saturated moss. This time when she got to the names carved in the fence, she knew who they were.

She tied a bunch of wildflowers together with a tough blade of grass and tucked them into a crevice in the post that bore the names of her family. She fingered the grooved lettering of their names—tracing the carving that her mother had made with a pocketknife. She noticed that Auntie Madeleine's name was not engraved there. That was a good thing.

From Kokum, Misko knew it was her mother who decided to create that memorial fence in honor of those who had gone to residential schools.

Although Kokum only shared bits and pieces, fragments of information, about her mom, she remembered Kokum's words one day: "M'girl, there are bad things that happen in this world. That school that your mom got sent to was one of those bad things," Kokum lamented. "Them people stole her ability to *trust*. That's how they crushed them. Never let them do that to you."

Misko shook her head as if to shake off all that was bad. She couldn't decide yet if this fence post was also meant to be the memorial for her mother—who left her at four years old and never saw her turn five.

Chapter Nineteen

A truck with a long horse trailer was parked outside the barn. Misko heard a man's voice. "Thomas! Get your ass over here!"

She couldn't help herself and moved closer to the barn, standing in the shadow of the door.

It was the man who'd whipped Mishtadim, Thomas's dad, Mr. Desjardins. He was tall and muscular with dirty blond hair that was going gray and he walked leaning forward. He had one of those big Adam's apples sticking out of his neck that moved up and down every time he yelled. He yanked hard on Mishtadim's harness, and Misko could see the bit cutting into the squealing horse's mouth.

"You didn't muck out the stalls like I told you to. You didn't get these horses out to pasture. What the hell did you do while I was away? Do I have to knock some sense into you, boy?"

"No, sir. I got most of the stalls cleaned. But you're back early and I didn't have a chance to finish—" Thomas turned to point and didn't see his father's arm come up, but when it was mid-swing, Misko yelped. And before she could hide, Thomas's dad yelled, "Who's there?" He strode up to the barn door, his eyes landing on Misko. "Who the hell are you?"

Thomas's eyes flashed, warning Misko to run.

She backed up, wondering how far she could get, but Mr. Desjardins was already at her side. His eyes narrowed and his lips were tight, thin lines. Misko's stomach lurched as her breathing became shallow. He grabbed her by the elbow, and she winced at the pain that shot through her still healing, bruised armpit. She looked up at him and a mental image flashed in her mind—the man who had slapped her in Winnipeg also looked like he'd gotten an apple stuck in his throat. The resemblance between the two men was chilling. Mr. Desjardins's violent grab only bolstered that bad memory.

"I said, who are you?" He turned and looked back at Thomas. "Is *she* why you're not getting your chores done? Hanging around with this Indian girl?"

Thomas got to his feet. "As if," he said, rolling his eyes. "Never seen her before."

Misko flinched at the sting of his words. He had just denied her existence.

His father dropped her arm and turned on his son. "Don't get smart or I'll swat that big mouth of yours."

Misko saw that Thomas didn't look too scared. He turned to Misko. "Well? You heard my dad. What are you doing here? Go back to where you came from. What do you want anyway?"

"Nothing." She spat out the word. "Nothing from *you*," she went on, and under her breath she added, "Thomas, don't let him hurt you."

"What's that, missy?" Mr. Desjardins roared.

"Nothing! I'm new here on the rez and I was—"

"New on the rez?" Mr. Desjardins repeated with a sneer. "Why would anyone come to that hellhole to live? You all live like squatters over there on that side of the fence. Most of your kind want to escape. Honest Injun," he chortled, holding up his hand like he was saying "How" from an old cowboy movie. "Now, why don't you mosey on back to your side of the fence?" he continued. "Before you go, did I tell you that I once knew an Indian guy from your side? I think his name was Charley Horse ... or was it Luke Warmwater?" He chortled some more.

Misko narrowed her eyes, held his gaze, and refused to flinch at his lame jokes. *Why are my people so often the butt of a joke? Why are we some kind of punchline in this country?*

"Ah. Well." He looked at Misko for a moment too long, his eyes softening. He opened and closed his mouth quickly as if shutting down something he'd regret saying. She stared back at him and could see he recognized something—*someone*—in her. He shook his head as if to fend off the memory like an irksome fly and turned to Thomas. "On second glance, she's kind of pretty, isn't she, son? Wouldn't blame you if you *were* hanging out."

Thomas flushed. "Don't worry, that'll never happen."

Suddenly, they heard the crunching of gravel behind them followed by the sound of an engine stop. Then a car door opened and closed, and when they looked, a little blond boy, maybe three years old, came scuttling toward them.

"Daddy!"

Misko looked at Thomas and saw his mean expression melt away. "Hey, Billy boy!"

Mr. Desjardins turned around and the little boy jumped into his arms. Mr. Desjardins hugged him for a second and then started roughhousing with the child as if he were a grown man. Billy fell down and started to wail.

"Billy!" Thomas reached for him, but his dad pushed him away. "Leave him be. Needs to toughen up after a month with his mommy." The sound of footsteps on gravel announced another visitor.

Misko looked behind her. A woman stood there—Mrs. Desjardins, she guessed.

The woman had a distant look in her eyes. She wore no makeup and she looked tired and faded like a shirt washed too often. She turned and walked toward the house without speaking, without comforting her little boy, and without saying hello to her older son. Her husband caught up to her and they walked inside together.

"Tee Tee," sobbed the little boy. "Tee Tee. Me hurts."

Thomas held the boy close. "It's okay, Billy. It was an accident. Come on now. Be a big boy for Tee Tee."

"Tee Tee?" Misko asked.

Thomas looked at her, surprised, as if he'd forgotten she was even there. "It's short for Thomas. He can't say my name yet, so he calls me Tee Tee. Now go away like I told you."

Misko felt hot all over. She gasped and held her breath. She wanted to say something hateful, for hate seemed to live here and it clawed at her like scavenging birds preying on the carcasses of the dead. But she said nothing.

Instead, she turned around and ran, half expecting to feel sharp talons digging into her scalp, halting her flight. She ran and didn't stop until she was on her side of the fence. She wanted to blow that fence down, but instead she turned and kicked it. She hated this stupid wooden barrier that was built to separate, and to keep *her kind* corralled like animals.

Chapter Twenty

———— ❊ ————

Misko was leaning against the fence, watching starlings rise, swirl, and circle in the sky. The sun was going down. It had been a few hours since her troubling encounter with Mr. Desjardins. As she often did, Misko turned her attention to the sounds of nature for comfort. She heard overtones in the wind and the chattering of poplar leaves. She soaked in the humming of insects through her pores; she could hear the buzz of a bee up close or the bark of a rez dog in the distance. She followed the outline of the trees on the horizon with her voice, following its dips and rises as though they were musical notes. She listened to the natural world as if her entire body was one giant ear hearing nature's orchestra.

Thomas found her and broke the magic of the moment by speaking. "I know you're not *Indian*. I know you're Ojibway, Ani-shin-aabe, okay?"

Startled, she responded sarcastically, "Way to interrupt the moment."

Thomas climbed over and then leaned against the fence beside her with his long legs stretched out in front of him. "I'm sorry. My dad's . . . you can't understand."

She turned her body away from him and said, "You're on Indian land over here, you know."

He glanced around, seemingly surprised that he was now on *her* side of the fence. He hadn't really noticed that he had climbed over. "This here is the same fence that my dad told me never to cross, and his dad's dad told him never to cross, and so on down the line."

Misko slid her hands along the surface of the fence and faced Thomas. "Know why this fence is here? I've figured it out. It's not to keep us in. Nope. It's to keep the hatred and racism out. Out and over there with you and your dad where it belongs."

"I don't hate—"

Misko cut him off. "You don't, huh? Sure sounded like it back there."

"No, Misko, I—"

"Oh, so you remember my name now? I thought that you didn't know who I was?"

A small snipping sound like he'd cut himself slipped from Thomas's throat. "I meant you don't understand what he'd do. If he thought that I knew you, he would've said even *worse* things back there. I know the way he talks about Indian people, I mean . . . Indigenous people, and it's downright wrong. I mean, a son isn't supposed to feel embarrassed by his own father—but I *am* ashamed of him."

"He's what you call a racist, and I never ever want to hear his voice again! And he's a big bully, too," Misko declared, crossing her arms. She looked at Thomas's hurt expression. "But I get it." She rolled her eyes. "You were protecting me back there."

"Yes, I was." Thomas's relief lasted only a second. "I know you're being sarcastic, but I didn't want him to think that we're friends."

"Are we, you know, friends?"

"Well, I sure thought so. I mean, I wouldn't let any ol' girl yell at me the way you do."

She suddenly felt flustered; to avoid his gaze, she took an elastic from her pocket and tied her hair in a ponytail.

"Hey, can I see your hand for a minute?" he asked. "Don't worry, I'm not going to bite you."

When she put her hand out, he pretended to bite it, making a growling noise. Giggling, she pulled it back. When she gave him her hand again, tentatively, he held it gently in his, the touch of his skin warm and electric against hers. "You know, you can tell a whole lot about a person by the lines in their hand." He studied her palm. "You see this long line here—that's your lifeline. You're going to live a long life."

"Oh, that's original," she quipped.

"You see how your lifeline isn't broken? That's a good thing. And this line here means your life's about to change."

"Spoiler alert—it already has. I'm here, aren't I?" She paused. "How do you know all this anyway?"

"My grandma taught me. You see here," Thomas said, tracing the horizontal lines on her wrists. "These are called bracelet lines; yours are thick and straight, and that means good health. These little bumps here on your fingertips mean that you're very perceptive. And this line here is your heart line. It looks like you're going to have a great love in your life."

She pulled her hand away and hurried to change the subject. "Why is your dad so mean to you anyway? To you and your mom and Billy?"

He pretended not to notice her discomfort. "I guess it's the way he was raised. My granddad beat up on my dad. *Broke* him, as you say. I guess my granddad broke everything in his life—broke his horses, beat his wife, beat his kids, and kicked the dog. It was dead wrong. Now my dad does the same to us."

"But your mom didn't do anything even when Billy fell. She didn't—"

Thomas interrupted her. "She *can't* do anything. She's scared of him. Shut-down. She's run away a few times but keeps coming back. Now she lives in Kenora, but I know she's planning to make a final break from him someday."

"Why don't you go live with her there?"

"Why should I?" Thomas snapped. His anger rose up quickly, but Misko could tell the anger wasn't about her. "This is my family's ranch. One day it'll be mine to run as I please. Like with the horses. Horses hate fear—you think I don't know that? They just want to feel safe. You think I *like* hurting them? It tore me up the first time I hurt a horse. But if my dad's watching, I *have* to break them. I have to *man up*, or I'm the one who gets the whipping." He waited for her to say something, but she just listened. He went on, "What you said the other day about breaking children? Well, I've been thinking 'bout it. And you're right. I don't know anything about those residential schools. But my dad, well—that's what he's been doing—to me, to Billy, and my mom. Trying to break us. Now, I know it's not the same as residential schools, not by a long shot." He sighed. "But when it comes to Billy . . ."

Misko felt her own anger bubbling up because she always had to explain how it wasn't the same at all. Residential schools were designed to kill the Indian in the child. Auntie Madeleine said that an entire legal *system* was set up to destroy our people, our culture, and to take our land. But then she saw Thomas's bottom lip quiver and decided to wait for the right moment to tell him all of this.

A large wedge of geese flew low overhead in V formation, honking, noisy like dogs barking in the sky. Hundreds more geese came and darkened the sky for a few more minutes. Misko looked up, leaning back over the fence, squinting her eyes. She could hear the beating of their wings, their powerful movement slicing through the air. It was one of the most beautiful sounds that she'd ever heard. She felt their wings split the air apart, and in her imagination, their current lifted her up and up, spiraling her into their loud wing song. And from up high, she could see the pines, spruce, rock, and shining water. Like a soaring bird, she saw the land. Everything shone, and everything was alive: the waters sparkled, the rivers carved the land like silver veins, and the ground seemed to rise and fall like it was breathing. And it was all so magnificent. In her mind, she started to fall, spiraling and twirling like a maple seed, and the geese flew down and caught her on their backs. Their soft plumage was like a nest that broke her fall as they honked, barked, and cackled their extraordinary goose song. They carried her down and gently placed her on the ground, and then she . . .

"Misko? Misko?" A voice broke through her reverie. Someone was shaking her back into real time. "Misko?"

She looked around, the geese now gone, and Thomas looked worried. "What just happened? You looked . . . like you were in a trance or something."

Should I tell him? Would he understand? Or make fun of me? But one thing she did feel was that a hard knot inside her chest broke open, came undone, and was released. She sat there quietly, just breathing, and Thomas took the cue and sat beside her without speaking.

After a few moments, Misko leaned forward and took Thomas's rough hands in hers, seeing his broken nails caked with earth. "I can read palms, too, you know," she said as she traced his calluses with her fingertips. "These little bumps here, they mean you're a hard-working ranch boy. And these nails, they mean someone needs a good bath." They shared a hearty laugh.

"Help me with Mishtadim?" Misko asked, quickly pivoting the conversation and looking directly into his eyes. "Train him so your dad doesn't . . . can't get rid of him."

"You're crazy! My dad won't let—"

She cut him off. "You said you'll run things differently when the ranch is yours—which is on Indian land, by the way, but we'll talk about that another time." She paused to see if he had caught what she'd just said. Not so much. She pressed on and stayed focused on the matter at hand, taking inspiration from the geese that flew overhead. "You see, Thomas, how the geese all take turns being in front and falling back when they get tired. The ones in the back cheer on the ones in front to keep them going. Someday, your dad *will* fall back and it'll be your turn to be out front. So start now," she pleaded. "Start right now with Mishtadim."

He looked up at where the geese had flown by and then back at Misko, nodding slowly. "He's going to be around this week. Got some new horses coming in. But next Wednesday he's off to a rodeo. Can't ride anymore himself but sure likes to brag about how good he used to be. That is, until he was beat out by an Indian cowboy."

Misko giggled but inside felt a big surge of hope.

Chapter Twenty-One

Misko counted down the days until Mr. Desjardins was due to leave again. She could hardly wait for Wednesday to arrive so that she could see Mishtadim again. The days seemed to drag on forever. Shoshana wasn't spending much time at Kokum's either, so the time stretched impossibly long.

On the weekend, Misko tried reading the paperbacks again, but it was hard with the days so warm. In a fit of boredom, she swept the floor and cleaned the cupboards in the kitchen. She even tried to help in the garden, but Kokum could tell that she was too distracted and gently shooed her away. Misko's thoughts were all over the map, clamoring and making noise in her head. Images of Mr. Desjardins kept appearing and dissolving in her mind, her body starting to feel the fatigue.

On Tuesday, no longer able to stay put, Misko had an urge that she could hardly contain. She remembered the kindness of Mr. Turner and that he had once helped her up onto the pony's back. *Would he help me again?* "Kokum, I'm going to the store. Do you need anything? I'm going to get something for supper tonight."

"Just a loaf of bread, dear."

Misko nodded, quickly deciding that she was going to get a few more things, although supper wasn't her real motive. Earlier, the blaring thoughts in her head formed into one especially nagging one and she really needed to talk to Mr. Turner. He knew about her grandfather, and she was feeling restless and determined to find out all that she could.

She meandered alongside potholes and a ditch swollen with water. Some children were splashing their feet in puddles, and muddy dogs were yapping and chasing each other. She felt lighter than she had during the past two days, and she skipped all the way to the store.

Mr. Turner was out front sweeping the walkway.

"Hello, Mr. Turner," she called. He waved and welcomed her in, and she followed him inside. From the freezer, she chose a package of hamburger meat and grabbed some buns, a tin of beans, and a bottle of ketchup from the shelf. "It's Sloppy Joes tonight."

Mr. Turner spoke at last. "Saw your grandmother yesterday. Told her she was fortunate. Not many young grandchildren come back to live, only to visit."

But I'm not coming back to live. There's not much for a kid to do here. And it feels sad without my mom being here. But Misko didn't say those thoughts out loud.

"Your grandmother—" He started but then shook his head. Misko watched as he started to organize some things behind the counter instead. *Why did he suddenly cut himself off?*

"Mr. Turner?"

He straightened out a display of gum and lip balms, sweeping away nonexistent dust with the back of his hand.

"You were going to say something about my grandmother?"

"She, ah . . . She told me about that horse you like so much. That's a very special horse."

"She told you about Mishtadim?" Misko had no idea her grandmother was paying such close attention.

Mr. Turner smiled. "Is that what you call him? That's a good name for a horse. She loves you so much, she—" He coughed and cleared his throat. "I know you have a special knack for horses, just like your mom," he said, his eyes searching her face, and she nodded solemnly.

"Mr. Turner, you seem to know a lot about folks around here, so I'm wondering—"

"Well, actually, my wife was the one who knew everybody's business 'round here, God rest her soul. Married almost 40 years. People ask how we stayed married for so long. I tell them it's because neither one of us thought about divorce at the *exact same* time," he said, laughing mischievously. "Seriously, though, I sure was lucky to have her as my wife for so many years." He paused for a moment. "How come you ask, Misko?"

"Well, Kokum doesn't talk much about my mom or my grandfather. But she says that you were friends with him."

"That's right." He nodded.

"I remember you helping me get up on a pony when I was a kid. You were really nice to me. Thank you for that and . . . Mr. Turner, I need your help again. Can you please tell me what happened to my grandfather? Kokum said you were friends since you were kids. I need to know. It's my history, too."

Mr. Turner patted her hand and took out two pieces of gum from his shirt pocket and offered one to her. She put the gum in her mouth in a second and began chewing, while he took his time, slowly unwrapping his piece and folding it in thirds before putting it in his mouth. "We were loggers. A handful of us from here, cutting and hauling trees across the ice. Back then, we sometimes used horses and dog teams, but we had started to use pickup trucks, too. We cut big blocks of ice for people for their ice houses, you know, for refrigeration." His voice was low and steady. "In between, we'd do some ice fishing. Nothing tastes as good as fresh pickerel over a winter fire." He turned to serve another customer at the counter and punched the numbers into the register. "That'll be $45.70, John-John." Mr. Turner turned back to Misko, who was looking curiously at the man. "Oh, that's John-John. He's called that because he says everything twice."

John-John smiled and replied, "True-true." Misko watched him leave, the door clanging behind him.

Misko turned back to Mr. Turner and smiled encouragingly at him.

"Now where was I? Oh yeah, we were on the ice that day in a pickup truck, and the ice didn't hold. Too close to a pressure crack, and well . . . the truck went through . . ."

Misko held her breath, wanting and not wanting to know the rest.

"Noodin . . . your grandfather was driving the truck and I was on the passenger side. The truck went through the ice on a slant like this," he said, tilting both hands to the left. "And the driver's side went down first. I was able to get out because I was closer to the ice surface. When your grandfather was finally pulled out of the water, it was too late. You only have a short time in ice-cold water before you die of hypothermia. I . . . I couldn't save him." Mr. Turner's eyes became watery. "Somehow, I was the lucky one on that day." Mr. Turner gulped down hard and cleared his throat, his teeth chattering as if still feeling the freezing cold on that terrible day.

Misko shivered. She hugged herself as if to warm up.

"I lost . . . I lost . . ." Mr. Turner covered his face with his hands, his voice trembling. Misko noticed that a few of his fingertips were missing. "Frostbite," he explained when he noticed her looking. "I . . . I lost my best friend that day." He lowered his head. "But your Kokum never wanted me to feel bad about what happened. She knows it was an accident and I couldn't save him. But it still haunts me to this day. I couldn't save him." He looked up at her. "You're lucky to have her as your grandmother. And I guess . . . she didn't want to tell you because she doesn't want me to feel bad for what happened. Because she knows that I do," he added. "I haven't been to visit her since, probably out of guilt, but one day, I will. Misko, I'm telling you all this because you asked and because I want you to know that your grandfather was the best man I *ever* knew."

Misko felt hot tears streaming down her cheeks. She could see everything happening on that awful day as he had described it. Other customers now started to arrive at the store, so she bundled up her few groceries, paid for them, and whispered, "Chi-miigwetch, Mr. Turner," standing on her tippy-toes to give him a shy peck on the cheek. She hurried out.

She ran all the way home, splashing mud up the back of her legs. Dogs followed for a while, barking, happy at what they thought was a game.

Misko stopped outside the door, closed her eyes, and let the sun poking through a cloud warm her face before entering the house. Kokum was sitting on the sofa. Misko crossed the room, put the groceries down on the kitchen table, and nestled in beside her. "I know about Mishoomis, my grandfather."

Her chin started to quiver uncontrollably and then she cried and cried. Kokum cradled her and whispered into her hair. "Shush-shush-shush. Little chickadee. Chickadee-dee-dee. Shush. Everything is going to be all right, my little bird."

Misko's dreams were short and intense that night.

As I walk across the clear ice, I hear a big crack beneath my feet. A huge zigzag moves across the ice. From beneath the ice, a man's face swims up and he reaches out with his hands. Some of his fingertips are chopped off. As he sinks down into the depths of the deep water lake, I gasp and I'm suddenly enveloped in darkness.

Chapter Twenty-Two

———◆———

*R*ow upon row of girls are lined up, and a man stands there holding a red apple in his hand. The girls are all screaming, so he belts them with one hard slap across their faces and they fall like dominoes, one after the other. The wallop stings their faces and leaves a red hand imprinted on their cheeks. The man gorges on the red apple, and his mouth turns red with blood that drips down his chin. When he swallows the rest of the apple, it gets stuck in his throat. He tries to gulp down hard, but instead the apple gets further lodged in his neck and stays there.

Hardly able to breathe, Misko woke up thrashing in the sheets, sweating profusely, her heart pounding. She just could not make sense of her visions. Despite being fully conscious now, her cheek started to sting. The dream fueled the memory of her near abduction and made her feel afraid all over again. She longed for her mother's comfort and feared that she was gone forever.

Shoshana had stayed over and slept like a log the entire night. Misko got up early in the dark and tiptoed around trying not to wake her. She heard rustling and Shoshana's sleepy whisper. "Where are you going?"

"Out. You'll have to wait and see. Go back to sleep," Misko whispered back.

"Let me come, too," Shoshana said, and in a snap she was out from under the covers, pulling on her jeans and sweatshirt.

"But what if Kokum needs you?" Misko reprimanded the girl for not doing the job she wasn't doing either.

Shoshana searched her face. "You don't want me to come?" She plopped herself down on the bed in a sulk— her bottom lip trembling—looking five years old.

"Don't say that. Just . . . I need some time to myself, and you'd be a . . ." *Distraction*. She remembered what it felt like when her aunt said those exact same words to her. She couldn't do it. "Fine. But hurry up."

"You're going to see Thomas, aren't you?"

"Shhh, do you want to wake up Kokum? What makes you think that, anyway?" Misko said, somewhat surprised.

"I saw you talking to him the other day."

"Okay, c'mon. First we have to get some miijim."

"Good idea, food!" Shoshana whispered excitedly.

Misko went into the kitchen and opened the loaf of bread that she had bought at the grocery store. She handled the bread like she was dealing cards. "Two for you, two for me, and two for Thomas." She spread peanut butter and jam on all six slices, wrapped them in wax paper, and grabbed a bunch of carrots from the fridge. "Thomas's dad is leaving today, but he's coming back soon, and that's important because . . . Remember the horse I told you about? Well, I'm going to help train him."

Shoshana's mouth fell open in surprise and Misko almost burst out laughing at her expression. "C'mon, let's go, ambe!" she said, and the younger girl jumped up, a tiny squeak escaping her lips.

Misko closed the door quietly and the two girls skipped down the steps and onto the footpath. Misko heard something rustling in the low bushes and put out a hand to stop Shoshana. She coughed, trying to scare whatever it was away. After a moment, a puppy bounded out, his tail wagging. She wondered if he was one of the dogs that followed her home from Mr. Turner's the previous day.

"Shoo," Misko said. "Go on home."

She crouched down to take a closer look at the puppy. He looked like he was wearing a little tuxedo. He was mostly black with a white patch on his chest and on his chin. He nudged his head under her hand and she felt his cold, wet nose.

"But you know he doesn't necessarily have a home, right?" said Shoshana. The puppy jumped up on Misko, his paws on her chest, licking her face. "Awww, so cute! He likes you! People always think rez dogs run wild," Shoshana complained. "Maybe 'cause they're not tied up all the time. Doesn't mean they aren't owned by someone."

Owned. There's that word again.

"Why do people want to *own* everything?"

"What do you mean?" Shoshana asked quietly.

"Why do they have to *own* everything, *take* everything, *break* everything? Like Mishtadim. He'll never be someone you can *own*. I can see it in his eyes. Mishtadim is still part wild, and I never want to take that away from him."

Misko took in a gulp of air and exhaled deeply, letting some of her frustration out on her breath. She stomped ahead—Shoshana half running and stumbling to keep up with her—as the puppy kept jumping up on the back of their legs. Misko wanted to push the puppy away, but as she did, her hand sunk into his soft, plushy fur, and her heart was caught by the light in his dark little eyes. Suddenly, she felt a calm wash over her and any anger dissolved. "So, whose little wolf are you going to be?" she said to the puppy playfully. Knowing it was a mistake, she ripped off a corner of her sandwich and he happily wolfed it down, wagging his tail endlessly.

"Now he'll never leave you alone!" Shoshana cheered.

Misko laughed, Shoshana joining her; their laughter was full of relief.

As the girls ventured on in the morning dew, the puppy followed along, nipping their legs with teeth as sharp as needles and tripping them up as he darted between them.

"What will you call him?" asked Shoshana.

"I don't think . . . actually I *know* . . . that Auntie Madeleine won't let me keep him."

Shoshana ignored her. "Oh! I know! You could name him Aniimoosh. That means dog. Your mom had a horse named Horse, so you can have a dog named Dog. It's perfect."

Misko wanted to say it was a silly idea, but for some reason, looking at Shoshana, so pleased with herself, and at the dog, so puppy happy, Misko laughed a big belly laugh. The sound waves of her laughter bounced off the land and rocks, and the tail end of her laugh laughed back. The girls erupted into fits of giggles when they heard their joyous echo. And then the tail end of their giggles giggled back.

They forged on, Animoosh running ahead, running back, barking his pleasure. The sun on the rise behind them magically made the barn's dull red paint brighten into a poppy-scarlet red. Thomas came out of the house and walked across the yard. They ran over to catch up to him. Misko noticed a bruise on his cheek.

"Hi, Thomas," called Shoshana. "What happened? Did your dad hit you?" When he didn't respond, Shoshana realized she had crossed a line. She quickly pivoted and pointed to the puppy. "This is Animoosh. Misko's going to adopt him."

Misko wanted to shush her, but Thomas leaned down and patted the dog's head and ignored Shoshana's question.

"Can Shoshana help us with Mishtadim?" Misko asked. With Mr. Desjardins having left this morning, the place already seemed more peaceful, even cleaner somehow. She guessed Thomas did a lot of tidying up while his father was too busy drinking and breaking animals to keep order.

"Tell him about your mom's pony, Mishtadim," Shoshana chipped in.

Thomas gazed at Misko quizzically. "What does she mean?"

Misko knew he'd make fun of her. "Well . . . my mom had a horse named Mishtadim. But I didn't know that. So when I renamed Brutus, I didn't know that . . . It was just a strange coincidence." She shrugged. "Seems weird, huh?"

"Yeah, you're weird, that's for sure," he said with a wink. He moved toward the barn. "My dad is supposed to be back in a few days. Never know when he'll show up though. But one thing I do know is that if Brutus isn't obedient and under control, my dad won't be able to sell him."

"What do you mean?" Misko demanded.

"My dad will just sell him for dog food or glue."

"Horses are sold for dog food or glue?" Misko asked in disbelief.

"Why are you so surprised? Everyone knows that!" Thomas exclaimed.

"That's terrible. That has to stop. I'll never treat Mishtadim like a beast of burden who can be thrown away, discarded like he was nothing." Misko shut her eyes, but the ugly image was still inside her mind. Instead, she opened her eyes and stared at the sun, burning the image out. "C'mon, let's get started."

Chapter Twenty-Three

———◦※◦———

Mishtadim was in his stall at the far end of the barn. Before they went to him, Misko stopped and said, "Thomas, he needs a proper name. It'll be our way of starting over if we give him a new name and not the one that your dad gave him. Brutus is not who he is." Thomas heaved a big sigh.

Shoshana touched Thomas's arm and added, "If your daddy's going to get rid of him, what difference does it make? It's just a name, right?"

"Fine. Two against one. You win. I'm caving only 'cause it doesn't make much sense," he said, scratching his head. "I just don't get what all the fuss is all about. It's just a name."

They were quiet as they walked toward Mishtadim in the barn. Misko saw that the stalls on one side were empty today. *Don't ask. Don't find out.* She took a deep breath and released it on the exhale. It was getting so much better. She rarely thought of the slap these days. Right now, she focused on Mishtadim and saw that the ground beneath him hadn't been cleaned, and she realized—but stopped herself from saying it out loud—that Thomas might actually be afraid of Mishtadim.

"I'll keep watch outside," said Shoshana.

"Good idea," replied Misko as she moved cautiously around the stall to Mishtadim's head. "Good morning, Mishtadim. Remember me?"

Mishtadim pushed his nose into her armpit and blew on her fading bruise. "Of course you remember!" He bobbed his head and whinnied. "It's okay. It hardly hurts today. Thanks for asking." She pulled a carrot from her pocket and extended her hand. "Good boy, Mishtadim. Beautiful boy, Mishtadim," she continued, and with her other hand, she scratched his muscular cheek.

Behind her, Thomas whispered, "Psst, that horse doesn't understand what you're saying. You know that he doesn't understand English, right?"

She whispered back, "It's not about the words. It's the feeling *underneath* the words that matters. Even if he doesn't understand my words, I can still communicate with him through . . . well . . . *feeling*. That's the best way to describe how we communicate."

"Oh." Thomas rubbed the back of his neck, considering that. "Okay, here comes the hard part," said Thomas as she watched him clip the rope to a halter. And with the *click* of the rasp, Mishtadim snorted and reared back.

"What happened?"

"Told you. We can't get near him. That sound makes him crazy."

"Mishtadim," she said softly, clearing her mind. "I know you're afraid, but we won't hurt you, Mishtadim. Everyone gets scared. It's okay, I'm here." She moved backward, away from the stall. "Maybe he's afraid of you, Thomas? Can you stand back a little? Maybe he'll let me halter him."

Thomas glared. "But you don't know how."

"So show me," Misko ordered. "On one of the other horses."

He cocked his head. "Huh. Not a bad idea. Watch and learn from the master!" He strolled down the row of stalls, walking like a big shot. "Maybe I should start you riding a bale of hay first so that you can get the hang of it?"

Now it was her turn to heave a big sigh and roll her eyes for extra dramatic effect.

"Oh okay, bad idea." He grinned. "Hey, Molly. How ya doin', girl?" Thomas opened the door and went in. "Ready for a walk and a trot today?

"See?" he said in a low voice, glancing back at Misko. "I'm standing on her left side and I'm letting her smell me."

"But why do you have to stand on her *left* side?" Misko asked. "I mean, she has two sides."

"This horse is trained from the left side. This horse ain't 'Indian broke', which means trained to mount on the *right* side."

"But wouldn't it be better if you could mount and dismount from both sides?"

Thomas ignored what he clearly thought was a silly question; Misko figured that he didn't really know the answer and watched him rub Molly's side with the curled rope.

"What are you doing that for?"

"So she gets the feel of the lead rope. And now I'm going to put it over her neck so I can steady her—hold both ends of the rope in my hand. Good girl. And now I can slip her muzzle through the nose band. Good girl, Molly. Watch how I buckle the halter. Atta girl." Thomas pulled the lead rope back and led Molly out of her stall.

Misko followed him out into the yard where he tied Molly to the fence. The other two horses, Star and Blaze, were already outside, swishing their tails to brush off flies. There was no sign of the shut-down mare. Misko shook her head to shake off the sad thought. She watched how the horses stood with their heads together, nattering, as if they were gossiping about another horse.

"Well, that looked easy enough," Misko said, motioning Shoshana to come over.

"It's only easy because Thomas has done it so many times, right Thomas?" Shoshana said, walking toward them.

Thomas smiled at her and gave Misko a dirty look. "She gets it, Misko. Why can't you?"

Misko ignored the dig. "Can I try? With another horse?"

They went back into the barn and Misko went through the same steps with a horse named Snickers. But she couldn't grasp the two ends of the rope in one hand in order to hold him and he kept squirming around. It was like trying to dress the antsy two-year-old she used to babysit back in Winnipeg.

Thomas laughed at her fumbling attempt.

"Oh shush," she said and started over. On her third try, she managed to grab the rope and slip on the halter.

"Not bad," Thomas said, nodding his head in approval, and Misko gushed with pride. "But Snickers is an old horse and well-trained," he added, as if he couldn't help knocking her down a peg or two.

"Let's get working with Mishtadim," prompted Misko.

"First you have to take Snickers outside. No point doing all that and not letting him have some fresh air."

Misko tugged on the lead. "Come on, Snickers," she said, clicking her tongue twice. The horse didn't budge.

She tugged again and the horse got a look in his eye as if saying, *You're not the boss of me.* He bared his teeth.

"Now that's just plain rude, Snickers!" Thomas told the horse. "Weren't you watching how I did it?" he asked Misko.

"Yes, I was, but—"

"Look, there's a right way and a wrong way with horses. I'll talk you through it one more time. Stand on Snickers's left side, up at his head, and hold the lead with your right hand." Misko obeyed. "Good. Now give a gentle tug and start walking. That's right. Always stay in the same place by his head. If you walk farther back, he can't see you. You might be a wolf, for all he knows."

As they walked out to the fence, Snickers cooperated and moved alongside Misko. The other horses whinnied at Snickers, and Misko felt like she'd gotten an A on her horse test.

"Atta girl," Thomas said. He was grinning, and Misko grinned back.

"Can I try on Mishtadim now?"

When Thomas and Shoshana started walking toward the barn with her, she added, "Alone, I mean. Can I?"

"I thought Mishtadim was stubborn, but you take the cake . . . Suit yourself." He walked over to the fence, and Shoshana followed him. They sat down in the shade beside Animoosh. "Listen, we'll be right here. Just holler if you need me."

Misko walked up to the barn door, stepping from the glare of sunshine into the soft, muted light of the barn. She scanned the rafters and inhaled the smell of horse and hay. Instinctively, she breathed in light and positivity, bucking any negativity from her mind. She had to let go of any anger and willed her mind to be clear, calm, and positive for Mishtadim. Since horses were really good at reading body language, her gestures also had to be clear, calm, and positive.

It was true that she didn't know much about horses. She tried to relax while urging the motionless Mishtadim to come closer. Taking a deeper breath this time from her back ribs, she exhaled all the other little bits of anger, fear, and resentment like debris. She inhaled again, and this time, she breathed in that afternoon on the shore with Nelson, Nimkii, Autumn, and all the other kids, remembering how the drumming was in sync with her own heartbeat. She was learning to inhale only oxygen and goodness and exhale the bad stuff.

Like a tree. Like mitig.

She opened her eyes and felt Mishtadim sensing her, watching her. She moved toward him and whispered, "Gizhawenimin, I love you."

He flicked his tail, whinnied softly, and stretched his head across the gate. Her heart swelled. "Good boy, Mishtadim." She held out her arm with the rope draped over it and offered a carrot with her other hand. She met his eyes softly and without saying a single word, she communicated from her mind to his. *I am here to help you. I will protect you, and I love you.* He received her energy, swung his tail freely, took the carrot, and chomped happily. Now standing on her tippy-toes, she rustled his mane lovingly.

Misko kept her voice low and gentle. "Mishtadim, my mother sent me to you. She's gone away, but I bet she knows your mare mom. I think I've seen them together in a dream. They would want me to help you." She lifted the rope and saw him pull back. She dropped her arm and rubbed the side of his cheek some more. She showed him the rope again and he backed away again. Every time she dropped her arm, Mishtadim seemed to relax. She gave Mishtadim another carrot. "That's enough for now, Mishtadim. You've done real good. We'll take a break now."

Chapter Twenty-Four

——◦✳◦——

The next morning, Misko and Shoshana got up early and raced up the hill to the barn to see Mishtadim. She brought a bunch of carrots with her to help speed up his training. They had no time to lose. At one point, Mishtadim plunged his nose into her pocket, rooted around, and helped himself.

"Don't tell me you're feeding him carrots again! That's a bad habit, Misko," Thomas scolded.

"I didn't know that you were up already," she said, a bit startled.

"Horses should behave without always getting a treat. Makes them sulky."

Misko watched as he walked Star and Blaze in clockwise circles, drawling out the commands "walk on" and "trot" and "turn," making the horses stop and start and change direction. "It's called longeing," he explained.

Misko tried the commands herself. "Taaa-rot! Eeeeee-see!" Thomas and Shoshana collapsed in giggles.

Thomas let Misko mount Star and led her around the corral until she felt brave enough to canter him by herself.

"This is going to be the best surprise ever when your dad gets back!" Misko said enthusiastically as he helped her down.

"What do you mean?" Thomas asked.

"Once we've trained up Mishtadim. Won't he be surprised?" Misko exclaimed.

"Doubt it."

"Why not? You don't have to tell your dad that I helped. He'll be real happy once he finds out that *you* finally trained Mishtadim, won't he? Can't you try talking some sense into him?"

"I don't think there's enough words for that. You've met my dad, right? And there's something you haven't thought about. As soon as he sees Mishtadim's trained up, he's gonna try to sell him. My dad needs the money. If he can get some cash for him, you know, *ka-ching*."

He was right. She hadn't thought about that. Her mind raced. "But he'll at least go to a good home, right? I mean, he's so beautiful. Someone will want him and take good care of him, right?"

"Yup, for sure," Thomas replied half-heartedly.

"I bet lots of people would want him," Shoshana chimed in encouragingly. Misko shook off her gloom.

Out of the corner of his eye, Thomas observed the horse. "You see Star's back leg? The left one? See how it's relaxed? That means he's not worried or afraid."

"Why can't you do that with Mishtadim?"

He shrugged. "He doesn't feel safe, I suppose. No imprinting at birth. Not by his mare mom or any people. When they caught him, he was wilder and madder and more scared than all of the other horses put together. That horse has spirit, I'll give him that much. He was so riled up he bit my dad and then my dad whipped him. Since then, no one's really been able to get near him."

At the mere mention of his dad, Misko cringed and exhaled with force.

"What's imprinting?" asked Shoshana.

"That's when the mare licks and rubs her newborn. The foal bonds with her and knows he's a horse. He knows her sounds and her smell. He knows she's his mom. And we sort of do the same thing with the foal. We rub the foal all over, so it knows a human won't hurt him. That kind of thing. You build trust that way. If we spend the time, this horse can learn to trust again."

"We *can* spend the time," Misko interrupted. "He just needs to feel that we understand him, that we care about him. Mishtadim hasn't had a chance to build trust. He didn't bond with his mom long enough 'cause she died and then your dad beat him. How's he supposed to trust anyone?" She couldn't keep the disgust out of her voice. "No wonder . . ." She jumped up suddenly, ran into the house, and got a banana from a fruit bowl in the kitchen. She ran back to the barn and paused at the door, remembering her ritual before meeting with Mishtadim. *Breathe in, breathe out. Breathe in, breathe out. Breathe in, breathe out. Exhale.*

Mishtadim was watching for her. He nickered softly, and when she held out the rope, he didn't pull away. He chomped on a piece of banana and Misko rubbed his torso with the rope. He was learning to trust her more and more. She talked to him and soothed him with her soft sounds of *sha-sha-sha* and *mishta-mishta-mishta.* Her gentle tone seemed to calm his horse heart as much as it did her human heart. She communicated from her mind to his without any words: *I'm here to help you. I want you to know that you're not owned by anyone. You can still be wild when you want to be. You can still run like you were born free. I love running, too, Mishtadim.* And then, like that first day, her arm magically rose up, light as a feather. She slipped the rope gently over his neck and passed the end of the lead rope under his neck with her left hand. She pulled the two ends together and while speaking softly, she clipped the rope gently to the halter so that the *click* was barely audible. He didn't move at all. "Good boy, Mishtadim," she said, giving him a well-deserved scratch in the space between his eyes. He blew into her braid.

"Ah-hey," she whispered to him. "Ah-hey, Mishtadim," she repeated, and she put her arms over his back, leaning her weight against him, smelling him, listening to his breathing, matching her breath to his. "Mishtadim, gizhawenimin, I love you. I'm staying. Hear that, Mishtadim? I won't leave you. I'm staying." She couldn't believe that those words came out of her mouth—*but staying on, as in a few more weeks? Or staying on as in going to school here next year or what?* Saying those words made it somehow feel very real. And what if she *were* to stay? *But how could I ever leave my friends in Winnipeg? Won't Auntie Madeleine be lonely without me? What would my coach say about me not being on the track team next year? He needs me to help the team win.*

She felt the slip of Mishtadim's hip as his back leg relaxed. She felt his weight shift as he leaned into her. Something deep welled up inside of her like never before. Her hands started to shake as a surge of electricity looped through her, haltering her to Mishtadim. The energy flowed into her blood, her bones, and every muscle like an electrical current.

When she trusted her instinct to move, she stepped beside his head as Thomas had told her to and gently pulled on the rope. Side by side, the horse and girl walked the length of the barn, his head bobbing up and down as he walked. They walked as if they were two peas in a pod, cut from the same cloth, girl and mishtadim. At the barn door, she paused, waiting for his eyes to adjust to the light outside. She saw Shoshana holding on to a wiggly Animoosh and she saw the surprise on Thomas's face.

"Whoa! How did you do that? How did you ever get to talk horse so well?" exclaimed Thomas.

"Dunno. I just try to see everything from his point of view. I build trust with him one step at a time."

She walked Mishtadim to the fence, and when they stopped, the horse leaned into her. "That horse is giving you a hug," Thomas said softly. "Since they don't have hands to hold or arms to give hugs, they kind of *lean in*. That's what Mishtadim is doing—he's giving you a horse hug."

Misko nodded but didn't have any words. Her eyes welled up. She took a few steps and, trembling, plunked herself on the ground and wept.

She walked home with Shoshana that evening, and their steps were slow. Despite the day being so perfect, a cloud of worry hung over Misko as she thought about the inevitable. There was so little time left before Mishtadim's shaky fate was decided. She prayed in her mind as they walked. *Please, Creator, Gichi Manitou, please take care of Mishtadim. Please keep him safe.* She felt so happy being with him that it reminded her of her mom's love for horses, too. Shoshana squeezed in closer to Misko as they walked together watching the sky grow dark as they made their way home.

Chapter Twenty-Five

M isko woke up to the pungent smell of wet sweetgrass. It was as if someone had put smelling salts under her nose. She sat up, looked around, but no one was there.

"Misko, Misko," Shoshana called, knocking on the door. "It's Thomas; he's outside and he looks scared."

"What time is it?" she asked.

"It's early, six o'clock."

Misko dressed quickly and hurried outside. Thomas was sitting on the step, Animoosh beside him, licking his face.

He turned, and she saw the cut on his lip.

"What happened?"

"My mom and Billy are still in Kenora, but my dad got home late last night. He'd been drinking all day and he came after me. I showed him what we did with Mishtadim. Showed him how we even did some groundwork with him. And you know what? He wasn't happy at all. He was mad. Mad at me for treating that horse in a kind, gentle way. He got his whip and went out to the barn and pulled Mishtadim into the arena."

"What did you do, Thomas?"

"I tried to stop him, but he turned around and hit me and knocked me to the ground. He was yelling, yanking, and swearing. He cracked the whip and then whipped Mishtadim. And Mishtadim screamed and pinned his ears back flat like he does when he gets really, really mad. I could see in his eyes that he wasn't going to take it anymore."

Misko felt woozy. "Then what happened?"

"Mishtadim reared up and knocked my dad down, and he hit his head when he fell. He got a big gash here." Thomas pointed to his forehead. "Of course, he's too stubborn to go to the doctor to get stitches. He said that he's had it with that horse and he's going to put him down. He's going to take him to be slaughtered!"

Misko gasped for air. She couldn't breathe and could see it all happening in slow motion—the whip coming down on Mishtadim's flank, the slap across her face from her past, and Thomas getting hit by his dad all combined into one big, painful sensation. Her breathing became irregular and shallow again, but she quickly remembered how to calm herself down. She started to talk to herself the way she did with Mishtadim: *It's okay, everything is going to be all right, just breathe. Inhale, exhale.*

"Misko, I'm afraid of what my dad might do to Mishtadim. We need to get him away from here."

"Your dad probably does love you deep down," Shoshana chimed in.

"Well, he sure has a crappy way of showing it," Misko countered.

Thomas imitated his father. "I love you, Thomas. *Punch.* I think you're great, Thomas. *Kick.*" Then he chuckled sadly.

"Thomas, come inside and we'll figure something out."

He shook his head. "It's too late, Misko."

"Then"—she had to think fast—"we'll run away!"

"We?"

Shoshana covered her mouth with her hand. Her eyes moved wildly from Thomas to Misko.

"You can't stay here," Misko explained. "Your dad will find you. And I can't let Mishtadim down either. I can't break my word to him. Kokum says a promise is something that you never break. We have to go and get Mishtadim *now.*" She stomped her foot and snorted.

"Are you crazy? You want to steal a horse from my dad?"

"Not steal. Just borrow, on loan. Until we figure something out."

Thomas cleared his throat. "How are you going to do that?"

Misko didn't know. All she knew was that she had to get Mishtadim away from Mr. Desjardins. As soon as possible. The horse only trusted her. She looked at Thomas sitting on the step, sniffling, looking so small and broken. She had to do something.

"Just wait here," she pleaded with him. "You stay with him, Shoshana. I'm counting on you," she said and walked inside the house. Misko grabbed a pack of matches from the kitchen and came back outside.

"Meet me at the fence," she whispered to Thomas, her eyes serious.

"Shoshana, take the puppy with you. I don't want him to follow me. It's important." Misko was thinking of Mishtadim's fragile trust, not wanting to startle him with a dog that might feed off the excitement. It was important to keep everyone as calm as possible.

Shoshana nodded, her eyes large and serious. She whispered into the puppy's fur, quiet words that said everything was going to be okay. Misko pretended that she didn't pick up on the tremble in the girl's small voice.

"I still don't think this is a good idea," Thomas said. He looked terrified, no longer the mouthy boy she had met several weeks ago.

"Got any better suggestions?" Misko asked and turned around to leave.

She could see her own breath in the fresh morning air as she sped toward the barn. She loved to look down and see how lean and muscular her legs were. They were becoming so strong.

Although she didn't have a clear plan, she knew she couldn't falter. She had to stay focused, calm, and determined. There was no room for error. She just had to keep moving.

When she finally approached the barn, she slowed down and looked around carefully. There was a chance that she'd encounter Mr. Desjardins now that he was back, but from what Thomas said, his father tended to sleep late following his binges.

Misko opened the barn door gently, inhaling the familiar happy smell of the animals inside. There was warmth coming from the stalls and the horses were already awake. She walked to the end stall where Mishtadim stood, his ears pricked forward, recognizing her familiar steps. His quiet, low-pitched whinny made Misko's heart skip a beat. She spoke soothingly to him and grabbed the halter from the hook outside of his stall. She had to be extra careful not to startle him in any way. She put it on him very carefully so that he wouldn't hear the click.

Mishtadim followed her out to the arena. She noticed that he became anxious again, his skin prickling in waves across his body. The horse turned around, looked down at the ground, and pawed cautiously with his hoof at a dark figure. When he lifted his front right leg, so did the dark figure. When he swished his tail, so did the dark figure— Mishtadim was trying to make sense of his own shadow. It finally clicked for Misko that the horse might be a little bit afraid of his own shadow. She instinctively put her hands on Mishtadim's head and turned it toward the sun. He shook his head as if trying to get rid of an itch in his nose and then his body softened.

She summoned up her own courage and stepped up on an overturned galvanized bucket while holding on to Mishtadim's mane. She lay on her belly straddling the horse's back, her arms and legs dangling on either side of him. She waited there until Mishtadim was comfortable with her weight on him. She whispered what she was doing and then gently swung her legs around and sat up. To her amazement, Mishtadim stood absolutely still. He gave no reaction. No biting or kicking or snorting.

Slowly and steadily, Misko rode on Mishtadim's back to meet Thomas at the fence. She saw him perched on top of the fence post waiting for her. When he saw her riding Mishtadim, his mouth fell open, and his eyes went round and wide as saucers. "Whoa, you're riding him! You're doing it! You're riding Mishtadim!"

Chapter Twenty-Six

———◆※◆———

Sitting up high on Mishtadim, Misko could see a stand of trees in the near distance. They had to get away fast to save Mishtadim's life. She stretched out her hand to Thomas. "C'mon, get on. We don't have any time to lose."

"It's okay," he said, refusing her offer in a small voice.

"C'mon," she said again. "Get on. He's not going to bite you."

"I'm not so sure about that," Thomas said weakly.

"Are you *afraid* of Mishtadim?" she asked.

"No, of course I'm not afraid of . . . him—"

"C'mon, Thomas. We don't have much time."

Thomas stepped toward Mishtadim, and the horse stepped back before letting out a forceful snort.

"You see, I told you! He won't let me."

She held on to Mishtadim's mane as Thomas tried again, and the horse stepped back again. "There's no way I'm getting on that horse. No way." Thomas shook his head.

"Let's go, Thomas. We have to boot it."

"Running away isn't going to help, Misko."

"Do you have any better ideas? C'mon, we'll go where your dad won't be able to find us. Like in the bush way over there."

"I thought you had a plan."

"It's as good a plan as any."

"But what are we going to eat?"

"We'll eat roots and berries and stuff."

"What? We're going to eat twigs and bark?"

"And we'll make a shelter. I brought some matches to make a fire," she said, hearing her own voice trembling.

"Misko, this is nuts! I can't just run away."

"Listen, Thomas, I'm tired of hearing what you *can't* do; tell me what you *can* do!"

She threw her leg over to one side and gracefully slid down the horse's side. Once back on the ground, she took a few deep breaths. "And what about Mishtadim, eh? What's going to happen to him?"

Thomas sighed. "I promise I won't let my dad hurt him."

"You know you can't stand up to him. You're afraid of your dad, you're afraid of Mishtadim—I bet you're even afraid of your own shadow!"

"I am not!"

"You are, too! Scaredy-cat!"

"I am not! And what about you, huh?"

"What about me?"

"You run away from everything when you're scared . . . just like your mother!"

"You take that back." She clenched both fists and stepped toward him. Mishtadim whinnied nervously.

"You can't run forever, Misko."

"Yes, I can."

"All right, maybe you can, but that's what you'll become. The girl who always runs away from everything!"

His words stopped Misko dead in her tracks. He was right; she did want to take off, run away, flee. But, this time, something shifted inside her, rearranged itself, and clicked in her mind. *Why should I be the girl who runs away? I didn't do anything wrong. Am I running because I'm afraid?* She pictured all of the running in her mind. Her mother and all the little boys and girls running away from residential schools, and her own running away from the predator who tried to abduct her. There was so much fear and so much running. *It just isn't fair that we have to run away like victims on our own land.*

Right then and there, Misko took a bold step. She decided not to let her fear take control. There would be *no more running away*. Instead of running and giving into the fight-or-flight response, she'd find a way *through. I'll take*

slow steps in the right direction rather than run the wrong way.
But how will all of this work?

Thomas lowered his voice, and his words were measured: "I will stand up to my dad. And for your information, I know what he's most afraid of."

"And what's that?"

"He can't stand being alone. He needs me to be his shadow, to follow him everywhere. Someone he can walk all over. Even to . . ." Thomas's voice faded and he swallowed hard.

"Even to what?"

"To have someone to break." He gulped.

"I won't let him this time," Misko said. "And he won't break Mishtadim either. Now it's two against one."

Thomas nodded. "You're right. We won't let him hurt us."

"But, Thomas, you know that your dad will say the right things, do the right things—for a while. He'll get you home, cook your favorite meal, and then after a few days, he'll be right back to his old self again."

"Then I . . . I'll let him know that this time . . . *I mean it.* He'll be left alone with no one to run the ranch with him. I'll tell him that I'm going to cross that stupid fence once and for all and never come back."

"But you said that no Desjardins has ever lived on our side of the fence."

"That's right. I'll be the first, and he'll lose me . . . to the very people that he . . . despises."

"Hmm, this just might work," Misko said thoughtfully.

"It *will* work," Thomas replied with a sniffle as he turned away to wipe his eyes.

She put her hand gently on his shoulder. "Hey, are you . . . *crying*?"

"Of course I'm not crying. It . . . it's my a-allergies."

She turned him around and looked deeply into his eyes. "Do you promise? You won't let your dad hurt you or Mishtadim?"

"I promise."

"Cross your heart and hope to die?" She made a little *X* on her heart.

"Cross my heart and hope to die." He mirrored her motion, putting an *X* on his own heart.

"Help me up?" she asked, and Thomas came closer. Misko could feel him trembling a little. She knew that horses could detect fear, but this wasn't just plain old fear. It was more of a fiery excitement *mixed* with fear. Thomas interlocked his fingers to provide a boost for Misko's foot. Mr. Turner flashed in her mind as she remembered when he gave her a leg up on a pony when she was little. *People think kids don't remember kindness, but we do.* She held on to Mishtadim's mane, stepped into Thomas's hands, and launched herself gracefully, dancer-like, over the horse's back. As before, the horse stood perfectly still. She gently pressed her heels against Mishtadim's sides, tugged on the harness, and rather than saying "giddy-up," she said gently, "When you're ready, Mishtadim." The horse started to move and Thomas followed on foot. They walked back home together without saying a word, a girl on a horse and a boy beside her.

As they approached the fence, Thomas scrambled over the wooden barrier. He said, "I'm going to take Mishtadim with me and run ahead to talk to my dad. He must be awake by now."

Misko slid off Mishtadim and hesitantly passed the leather straps to Thomas. He clutched them, his knuckles turning white from pressing too hard.

"Will you be okay?" she asked. "Promise me that nothing will happen to Mishtadim."

"I promise. I know just what to say to my dad," he called back as he stomp-ran into the distance with Mishtadim somewhat reluctantly trailing behind.

Chapter Twenty-Seven

M isko paced frantically around her room. Ever since getting home, she'd been worrying about Thomas with his father and Mishtadim. She wanted to talk to Kokum, but she wasn't sure what to say or how to explain everything. There had to be another way—she just couldn't picture Thomas standing up to his bully of a father, someone who just couldn't see what they were trying to achieve. It was as if he wore sunglasses that made things look dark and gruesome everywhere he looked. *He needs a new prescription.* She felt her flight response kicking in and was ready to bolt. She just didn't know how to contain all of this energy.

Finally, she had enough of her own nervous company and decided to do something about it. She decided to *speak up*. She knocked on Kokum's bedroom door. When her grandmother opened the door, Misko burst into tears and fell into her arms, her whole body shaking. The entire story came out in hiccups and frantic starts and stops as Misko relayed the fate of Mishtadim. She felt the anxious energy leaving her body, but she still was full to the brim with unrelenting thoughts. Her mind was getting all tangled up.

Her grandmother smoothed her hair and whispered to her, "There, there," and patted a spot beside her on the bed. Misko leaned her head on Kokum's shoulder and closed her eyes. The sound of birds outside penetrated the window, and in the distance someone who sounded very much like Shoshana was singing and laughing.

"M'girl, I'm glad that you told me what happened," her grandmother said sweetly. "I know that it was hard. Bizindawishin. Listen to me." Kokum gently nudged Misko to sit up. Her voice sounded more serious than ever before.

"I want you to stay right here. I got to go and see Mr. Turner about a few things. But I don't want you leaving the house in case that boy comes back."

Instead of Thomas, it was Shoshana who came by for a visit. She brought some groceries and told Misko that she had run into Kokum at the store. "Mr. Turner and Kokum were whispering and didn't want me listening in, but I heard that it had something to do with your horse."

Chapter Twenty-Eight

———❋———

M r. Turner's old Ford truck kicked up a trail of dust on the dirt road leading to Mr. Desjardins's ranch. Seated beside the older man in the pickup was Misko, squinting to make out Thomas in the distance with his father. The truck pulled up the gravel driveway and screeched to a stop. Thomas's father swung around. "Now who the hell is that?"

Mr. Turner turned off the engine and climbed out while Misko got out from the other side. She could hear what sounded like a shouting match between father and son.

"I'm telling you, I can train Mishtadim . . . I mean, Brutus," Thomas screamed.

Mr. Desjardins rushed to grab the horse's halter, but Thomas ran up and blocked his way, and the man froze, his eyes narrowing as he watched his son. Misko looked frantically at Mr. Turner, but he gestured for her to keep calm.

Thomas threw his shoulders back and turned to his dad. "You can't hurt the horse anymore. And you can't hurt me! You're not the boss of me!"

Mr. Desjardins spat out, "But I am, boy. As long as you're under this roof, you'll abide by my rules. It's me who puts food on the table and I'll remind you that this is my ranch and my rules, and you'll do as I say."

"Then I won't stay here . . . because I know you'll hurt me . . . and you'll hurt Mishtadim, too. That's his real name, Dad. It's *not* Brutus. You think I don't have anywhere to go, but I do." Thomas's voice went an octave higher, and he could smell alcohol on his father's breath as they stood close to each other, but Thomas didn't move.

"And where on earth are *you* going to go?" Mr. Desjardins laughed a hostile laugh.

Thomas closed his eyes. He took a big, deep breath, letting it fill his lungs, and then he exhaled. When he spoke his voice was no longer shaking. "I'm going to stay and maybe even live over there . . . on *that side* of the fence."

Mr. Desjardins scrunched his forehead and shook his head as if he didn't understand, as if he couldn't absorb what he just heard. He tipped up the brim of his beat-up cowboy hat, which covered the jagged gash that he never got stitches for. "What did you just say? What are you going to live with *those* people for?"

Thomas looked over to where Misko was standing, and her stare was unwavering. She gave him an encouraging nod and cheered for him with her eyes. Now emboldened, Thomas turned back to his father. "You mean *those* people who you hate so much? *Those* people who treat me how I deserve to be treated? *Those* people who don't—" He felt the slap before he even saw the back of his father's hand. The strike wasn't hard, but it was enough to send him stumbling, and he tripped over a rock and fell backward. Lying on the ground with the dirt grinding into his elbows, he felt hot all over, the shame burning and washing over him. His father stood huge and terrifying above him, his body blocking the sunlight. Thomas scrambled backward on all fours out of his father's shadow. And then he got up, clenching his fists into a white-knuckled grip. He tightened them so hard that his fingernails made bloody half-moon indents on his palms.

That's when Mr. Turner made his move. He was older but he was still a big barrel-chested man, a former logger just like Misko's grandfather. That's what Misko thought of as she watched him saunter up to Thomas's dad, standing a few inches taller than him. She saw Mr. Desjardins shrink a little. His Adam's apple went up and down. Misko had been instructed to stay near the truck, but she was itching to get closer to the action.

Mr. Turner stood and chewed his gum, all the while looking intently at Mr. Desjardins. "Do you know why

I'm here? No. Don't talk. I'll make this simple. I'm here to make you an offer. Now, I'm going to take that horse. And you're going to sell him to me. I know you need the money and everyone around here knows that you can't pay your bills. You're in debt. So you see, I'm doing you a favor." He scrunched his nose, sniffing exaggeratedly. He sounded calm, his voice steady and low.

Mr. Desjardins opened his mouth to speak, but Mr. Turner held up his hand to stop him. He continued, "I remember you and your father coming to my store when you were a young whippersnapper. Back then, you didn't have all of this . . . this *hate* inside of you. But now I can plainly see that you suffered at the hands of your own father. And I'm sorry for that. I can see that all that hurt is still inside of you like an old fever. This much I know, hurt people *hurt* people. You blame that horse for everything that's bad in *you*. And you blame your son, too, but that doesn't give you the right to abuse that boy. Only a coward hits a child, and I won't stand for it. And you'll have to deal with me next time." Mr. Turner spat out his gum and held Mr. Desjardins's eyes.

Mr. Desjardins looked away, speechless.

Mr. Turner sighed. "I'm asking you man-to-man to leave this boy alone and get some help—for yourself, too. You're going to lose your ranch if you don't get a hold of yourself. You should be an example to this boy. Not someone he has to be ashamed of."

Thomas's eyes nearly popped out of his head. He had never seen anyone stand up to his dad before. No one had the guts. His feelings were all mixed up. On one hand, he felt relieved and safe, and on the other, he didn't like that his father was being scolded. He wondered if he should say something to defend his father . . . but nothing that Mr. Turner had said was wrong.

Misko watched as Mr. Desjardins turned around, his head hung low. He walked slowly back to the house, waving his hand as if to send them on their way. He stopped and turned to look at Thomas. He shook his head from side to side and tipped his finger to his cowboy hat as if to say "so long." The boy didn't look away, and he didn't smile. He held himself taller than ever before. Mr. Desjardins jutted out his chin at where Mishtadim stood tied up to a post. "Just don't come crying back to me when that horse kicks your head in," he muttered, slamming the door behind him. They all stood there in silence watching the window shade's pull-ring sway back and forth.

Chapter Twenty-Nine

On her walk home, Misko went over in her head how Thomas had stood up for himself and had grown in a matter of minutes.

Skrrrrt, skrrrt, she suddenly heard; it was the sound of metal scratching against rock. It was coming from Kokum's garden. She followed the sound and there stood her grandmother with a small spade in hand.

When Kokum saw her standing there, she beckoned Misko to come closer. Misko walked over and threw her arms around her. "Kokum, I know that it was you. You made everything happen for Mishtadim. You stickhandled this situation like no one else could. I'm so . . . so *proud* to be your granddaughter. I . . . I love you, Kokum, gizhawenimin," she said, tears running down

171

her cheeks. With strawberry-stained fingers, Kokum gently brushed Misko's hair off her face and wiped her tears. In her palm, she held a single strawberry: "Ode'imin, m'girl." She took her gardening knife and cut the strawberry in half. "What does it look like inside?"

"It looks like a heart," Misko said, sniffling.

"That's right, m'girl. Ode'imin. That's why we call it a heart berry. And it's good for the heart, too." Kokum smiled, placing her hand gently on Misko's chest. "What you carry in here is how you'll see the world. Ode, gide', gide'," whispered Kokum as if activating Misko's heart with her words. Then Misko heard the *thump-thump* inside her chest as though hearing her own heart beating for the first time. "M'girl, keep a good heart, a good mind, and good hands in everything you do. And all will be good."

"I promise," said Misko, rubbing her chest, which suddenly felt very sore. It was like her rib cage had somehow been opened up—not so much broken but more like something had hatched inside. She thought how her own heart and everyone else's have invisible lines, too. Heartstrings connecting us to everything and everyone and tugging on us to make us feel our own humanity. Even animals, trees, and plants have them. *Not just humans.* Then the sweetest memory bubbled up in Misko's mind from her early childhood. She remembered signing her name, like little girls do, with a little heart over each *i*. Miskobimizh. When she was little, she used to say that there were three hearts in her name. One heart was for her mom, one for her grandmother, and the last one was for her aunt. The warm memory brought back feelings of her little-girl love for life. And her own name shone and sparkled inside her mind: Miskobimizh. Unexpectedly, she felt the bounce again inside. It was like a little trampoline inside her chest starting to bounce once again with excitement and hope.

Kokum motioned that she was going back inside the house and Misko gladly followed her in. Kokum walked past the wall unit and said, "M'girl, I still don't have a picture of you. You were gonna bring me a school photo this year, 'member?"

"I . . . I did." She ran into her room and found the school photo that was pressed between the pages of a paperback. "Here you go, Kokum."

Kokum took the photo and looked at it lovingly. "That's a good photo of you, my beautiful girl. You look so much like your mother. It's like having her here again," she said, beaming. "But I think that your photo belongs over there now," she added, with a nod to the wall unit.

Misko walked over and scanned the faces of her family and relatives. She spotted the frame still occupied by the white couple with the beach ball and replaced that photo with her own. *Why do they get to come with the frame anyway?* She held up her reframed photo to show Kokum, and her grandmother's eyes shone with pride. She then placed it on the wall unit next to the photo of her mother with Mishtadim, her pony. She stepped back for a moment to get a better perspective of herself among all of her relatives. She took a deep breath and exhaled. *Family*.

Kokum went into the kitchen to make some tea, and Misko lay down on the sofa, intending to rest only for a moment. But she drifted off to sleep, hearing her grandmother puttering around and the *neep, neep, neep* of little birds and the scampering of squirrels up and down red pines.

Grandfather Noodin is waiting by the shoreline in the big birchbark canoe. A beautiful woman with flowing black hair appears and extends her hands, her bracelets covering her scarred wrists, the gemstone missing as before. As Misko holds out her hand, the woman pulls her into a big bear hug. It is the warmest, most energizing embrace she has ever felt in her life. It's filled with so much love. Her mother speaks only with her eyes. "My sweet daughter, I will always be with you. Never forget that I run in your blood. Never forget me." Her mother smiles and her eyes look like two half-moons. Then, Grandfather Noodin stretches out his hand and her mother steps into the canoe. As they paddle into the distance, they travel upriver in the spirit canoe that goes straight up into the sky.

When she woke up, she still felt half asleep from the dream, but she knew that her mother was on her spirit journey, traveling along Jibaykana, the Milky Way, the river in the sky.

"Wake up, m'girl." Her grandmother's soft voice broke through the fog of her half-asleep state. She realized that her head was now on Kokum's lap, and she was stroking her hair and whispering to her: "Miigwetch giibi' azhegiiweyin mbineshiwensim. Gizhawenimin. Thank you for coming back home, my little bird. I love you, my little chickadee."

Chapter Thirty

———◆※◆———

Misko opened the door wide and saw Thomas sitting on the step holding a wriggly Animoosh and Shoshana beaming at her. "Rise and shine, sleepyhead," Thomas cheered.

"I wanted you to know," announced Misko. "I talked to Kokum and there's no way that I can leave this place. I've decided to *stay.*"

"You're staying? That's amazing, Misko!" Thomas's face broke into the widest smile.

"Hurray! Woot woot!" Shoshana chimed in. Misko could see that Shoshana was biting the insides of her cheeks, bursting to talk more. Misko nudged her. "Go on."

"I won't be sleeping over as much now," Shoshana blurted out. "I mean you're here now, and I talked to my mom about feeling scared at night. She talked to another nurse about switching her shifts around." Misko put her arm around Shoshana and pulled her into a brief hug. "I'm proud of you, sis." She leaned her head against Shoshana's shoulder and felt her warmth as she relived Mishtadim giving her a horse hug over and over in her imagination.

"Can I get in on this happy moment, too?" Misko heard a familiar voice and turned around to see Mr. Turner standing there with Mishtadim.

"Mr. Turner!" Misko exclaimed, as she ran over to give him a big hug.

"It's high time that I came over for a proper visit," he said, hugging her back.

Misko nodded and smiled. She allowed herself to be distracted with Mishtadim, who whinnied, his eyes following her every move. She wrapped her arms around his neck and leaned into him. She felt a melody suddenly rise up inside of her. She closed her eyes tightly and re-membered her mother's lullaby in the dream. She hummed the lullaby—every note she could remember. She didn't realize that she was humming out loud until she saw Mishtadim swivel his ears, recognizing that this was his song, too.

"All horses need a song of their own," Mr. Turner said gently.

"Hey, I heard that once, too, so I tried it," Thomas added. "And you know what? It *does* calm them down."

It occurred to Misko that Thomas wasn't so tough after all. She wanted to tease him, rez-style. *And what horse lullaby did you sing for good ol' Snickers? "Hush-a-Bye, Baby, Don't You Cry"?* But she worried that he might get embarrassed and revert back to his tough-guy act. She could see that deep down he knew that he didn't have to break horses to make them love you.

Instead she said, "That's beautiful, Thomas. Everyone needs a song."

Mr. Turner gave Misko a big right-side-up horseshoe smile, crinkling his nose as the sun hit his shining eyes. "Yesiree, if you treat a horse with kindness, you get a horse that will give you absolutely everything. Now, you have to earn a horse's trust, but once you do, it's a beautiful privilege that you get to keep. And that there horse trusts you, Misko."

She felt a nudge at her side. "Ah, somebody's a little impatient," Mr. Turner said with a nod to the horse. She felt the rough-soft touch of leathery straps being placed in her hands. Mr. Turner nodded again and said with a smile, "Here's the reins. Take him for a walk."

Misko started walking, unhurriedly, and Mishtadim followed slightly behind her, his tail swinging freely. She paid attention to this magnificent animal's signals and his pace, and she could feel their hearts beat in sync. *Thump, thump . . . thump, thump.* As Mishtadim caught up to her, she watched the twitching of his ears and the rippling of his muscles on his flanks as he whinnied quietly in anticipation. She could tell that Mishtadim, too, wanted to walk gently beside the girl who loved him so much.

Chapter Thirty-One

The world looked a lot bigger atop Mishtadim as Misko rode along the fence. She noticed how alive his ears were, moving as they picked up sounds from different directions and then suddenly twitching forward again. *I so wish that I could see the world through your ears and eyes, Mishtadim.* She ruffled his mane lovingly. Suddenly, she noticed something that she hadn't seen before. There was a fence post in the near distance that looked like a carved totem or something similar. She steered the horse toward it and then slid gracefully off his back. She tied Mishtadim to the fence and walked up close to examine the post, her eyes squinting to make out the words. Her fingers searched the engraving as if touch could tell her something more. Her heart started to pound as she read the poem fragment:

Like a little bird,
I will come with a song
in the morning dew.

How beautiful, she thought. *There must be more.* She ran over to the next fence post and there was indeed more. She continued to read:

When you look up
at the sky at night,
I am the star who
shines brightest for you.

She pushed the tall grasses away from the post but couldn't find the author's name carved anywhere, not even initials. She clambered over to the other side of the fence; nothing was there either. She ran to the next post and then another, but they were all smooth with no carvings.

She walked back to where Mishtadim was standing, plopped herself down on the ground, and lay flat on her back. Looking up at the sky, she noticed the tall blades of grass all around her. They seemed to have encircled her, waving in the wind. A light breeze came up and they rubbed up against one another, murmuring, *Shhhshhh wiingaashhhhk.*

"Wiingashk," she whispered.

She remembered Kokum's words in the garden one day: "Wiingashk, sweetgrass, is good for memory; breathe in wiingashk, and you'll remember everything." She flashed back to her dream where she'd woken up smelling wet sweetgrass and thought someone had put smelling salts under her nose to wake her up.

She came back to the present and inhaled its sweet scent, and on the exhale, she wondered, *Who wrote these little poems?*

"Ninga, Mama," she whispered softly to herself. She lay there on her back some more before turning over on her belly. She folded her arms underneath her head and repeated, "Ninga, Mama." She shivered, and then her whole body started trembling, and with a shaky voice, she cried, "Nin-ga, Ma-ma. Nin-ga, Ma-ma!" It all started to flow out of her. Eight years of pent-up hurt, anger, and missing her mom. Her chin quivered and she cried like she had never cried before, her tears pelting into the ground. She could hardly get the words out. "I—love—you—so—much, Nin-ga, Ma-ma."

As she wiped her nose with her sleeve, she thought, *The kids back in Winnipeg would say I'm a big sucky baby,* but she couldn't help herself. She tried to take a deep breath, but it got caught in her throat: "Nin-ga, Ma-ma, I mi-iss you so mu-ch." And then she started sobbing all over again. Her vision started to blur with her own salty tears. How she hated that tears came so easily to her. Her auntie said her vulnerability was a strength and not a weakness. But right now she sure felt like a big crybaby and a loser. Between her bouts of tears when there were moments of silence, Kokum's words wedged themselves into her thoughts. *Just because you lose someone, it doesn't mean that you stop talking to them.* Those words soothed her like a gentle wave caressing the shoreline. Like mashkiki. Medicine. Sniffling, she realized how profound and wise and loving her grandmother really was—she could talk to her mom no matter what and where.

She looked at her hand outstretched by her side. It was trembling as blood pumped through her veins. She marveled at how the color of the back of her hand matched the land, and she saw her mother's beautiful brown skin in her hands, too. She took a handful of earth in her palm and sifted the soil through her fingers. It reminded her of an hourglass, and she was hypnotized by the sands of time trickling through. It was somehow soothing to watch, and her breathing became slower, calmer. She was no longer sobbing. She blinked, and suddenly in her imagination, a woman riding a horse appeared in the distance.

She could make out flowing black hair and a strong body clad in a short buckskin tunic and buckskin footwear, inhaling the land through her feet. The woman rode with a hand drum slung over her back; a bear's claw was painted in red ochre on its deer-hide skin. The symbol of the healer. Misko couldn't see the woman's face, but she could hear her melody and her breath. Instinctively, she knew that this woman ran in her blood memory. She was from long ago, the old time, and also in the here and now, all at once. Then the image evaporated.

She inhaled the rich earthiness all around her and brought her dusty hand up to her own cheek. Getting up to her knees now, she saw everything quivering and swaying —buttercups, sweetgrass, Mishtadim's mane, treetops, and even her own hair blew in four directions.

A gentle wind came up and brushed her hair off her face. It reminded her of Kokum's soft caress and her words in the garden one day: "People call this *wind*, but we call it the *breath* of our Earth Mother." She could feel the loving breathy wind on her skin now. *Why can't people see and feel this kind of connection? Why can't people take that love in and feel it all around them?*

She took a big breath and exhaled. "Miigwetch, Gichi Manitou. I'm so lucky to have been born here with all this beauty around me, with all of my relations. Thank you for bringing me *home*, Gichi Manitou, my Creator."

She remembered the family bracelet that Kokum had drawn that looked like Bagonegiizhig, the Pleiades star cluster. "Way up there," Kokum had explained, pointing, stretching her bottom lip upward toward the night sky.

"Those stars up there are not just balls of gas—they're our relatives, too. Someday we'll go back there because it's where we come from. Everything comes full circle, and everything's round, m'girl. It's love that we came with, and it's love that we go with."

She remembered her mother's bracelet, too, with the missing gemstone. It suddenly clicked for her:

When you look up
at the sky at night,
I am the star who
shines brightest for you.

That was it, the missing gem. The brightest star was there all the time, shining like a luminous jewel in the sky. And although her mother was gone, Misko had found something here that made sense to her. She'd found her north star. She'd found home. People say that you can never return home once you leave, but that isn't quite right. It's more that *home never leaves you.*

She slowly stood up, walked over to Mishtadim, who had been waiting patiently, and threw her arms around his neck. He blew into her braid and leaned in. "You're home now, Mishtadim," she whispered. "And so am I."

THE END

Glossary

ambe: come

Ambe omaa: Come join us

animikii: the thunder beings

aniimoosh: dog

Anishinaabe: the human being

Anishinaabemowin:
   the Ojibway language

azhegiiweyin: when you
   go back; the act of going
   back; returning

Bagonegiizhig: translating
   directly to the Hole in the
   Sky, this is the cluster of
stars that is considered
the origin point for the
Anishinaabe (what is also
known as the Pleiades).

bineshiiwens: little bird or
   baby bird

Bizindawishin: Listen to me

Geezhigo-Kwe: Sky Woman

Gichi Manitou: the Great
   Mystery or the Creator

gidimaagendagozi: A pitiful
   condition or state

giibi: coming towards (prefix)

gizhawenimin: I love you

Jibaykana: The River of
   Souls, the Path of Souls
   (the Milky Way)

kawin: no
Kokum: Grandmother

manitou, nendamowin,
   wiiyiw: spirit, mind,
   body
mashkiki: medicine
mbineshiwensim: my little
   bird
miigwetch: thank you
miijim: food
Mishoomis: Grandfather
mishtadim: big dog or big elk
miskobimizh: red willow
mitig: tree

N'Dakii Miinan: our homeland
nichi: Friend
ninga: Mother
Nokomis Giizis: Grandmother
   Moon

ode'imin: strawberry
odikosiw: kidney
Odoobina'anangoog:
   She Holds Up the Stars
okonima: liver
onizhiishin: it is good;
   looks good

shiiwaniibish: dandelions

wiingashk: sweetgrass

zhingwaak: jack pine

Acknowledgments

I would like to acknowledge the endless inspiration of my homeland and people, the Teme-Augama Anishinaabe (People of the Deep Water) in Temagami, Northern Ontario, Canada. I am forever grateful to have grown up on a land with such incredible beauty, spirit, and imagination.

I am so fortunate to stand on the shoulders of many remarkable people who have influenced me for which I am forever grateful.

I would like to acknowledge and thank my wonderful family and the people who have encouraged and supported me along the way including Don Kavanaugh, Rick Wilks, Mary Beth Leatherdale, Kaela Cadieux, Catherine Baldwin, Jowita Bydlowska, and the entire Annick Press team. I would also like to acknowledge the generous support of the Ontario Arts Council, the Toronto Arts Council, and City of Toronto. Chi-miigwetch and much love to all of you for being part of this extraordinary journey.